MW00476553

Angels
in
Tesuque

To Mindy,

Thank you for
driving Cathy &
your Friends down
to S. Monica.

Very Warm Regards

Michael Glass
11/7/95

Angels in Tesuque

A Novel by
MICHAEL GLASCO

SANTA FE
New Mexico

T he events, people, and incidents in this novel are the sole product of the author's imagination. The story is fictional and any resemblance to individuals living or dead is purely coincidental.

Copyright © 1995 by Michael Glasco. All rights reserved..

No part of this book may be reproduced in any form or by any electronic or mechanical means including information storage and retrieval systems, without permission in writing from the publisher, except by a reviewer who may quote brief passages in a review.
First Edition

Printed in the United States of America

10 9 8 7 6 5 4 3 2 1

Library of Congress Cataloging in Publication Data:

Glasco, Michael, 1945-
    Angels in Tesuque: a novel/by Michael Glasco.
      p.   cm
    ISBN 0-86534-103-6 (hardcover). —ISBN 0-86534-071-4 (paper)
1. Indians of North America—New Mexico—Fiction. 2. Tesuque Pueblo (N.M.)—Fiction.
3. Young men—New Mexico—Fiction. 4. Pueblo Indians—Fiction. I. Title.
PS3557 .L3125A54   1995
813' .54—dc20   95-31303
                                                          CIP

Published by SUNSTONE PRESS
                Post Office Box 2321
                Santa Fe, NM 87504-2321 / USA
                (505) 988-4418 / orders only (800) 243-5644
                FAX (505) 988-1025

Illustrations by Pat Sreenan

PREFACE

The initial concept for this novel came to me at dawn on Christmas morning, 1993, while sipping coffee on the portal of my sister's home in Santa Fe. It was snowing, and the view stretches out to the hills surrounding Tesuque Pueblo. The idea came to me as suddenly and mysteriously as that unexpected snowfall.

I would like to thank my wife, Elizabeth, for her constant support and vital help in writing this novel. Also I would like to thank the following: my sister Marion Chambers for her encouragement, Joseph (Has-No-Horses) Hesbrook for sharing his essential insights into the spiritual and cultural world of the Native American Indian, and Lucy Chambers for her invaluable critiques.

—*Michael Glasco*
Dallas, Texas, 1995

FOREWORD

"I rubbed dust from the wall, and the ancient symbols came clear. They told us we are now in the fourth world, possibly the last. At the end of each world, a handful of people comes out to the next world, and saves it. These are the peaceful people, we call them; kind, gentle, truthful, humble people."

—*Thomas Banyacya, Hopi elder.*

ONE

Ben Touchstone, his young eyes crimson and swollen, drew the blanket closer to his chin and sighed, his breath freezing into circles on the window. His father, Ojo, had deserted them in the middle of the night without a word. Lit by the setting moon, Ben's small, pale face contrasted with the walls of the brown adobe house, nestled in a field on the edge of the pueblo.

He quietly watched as the wind from Taos raked snow from the topmost ledge of the mountain, then studied his reflection in the window; the straight nose, cobalt eyes, square jaw and sweep of straw-blonde hair across his forehead. He wished he'd been born otherwise, not with the curious bleached complexion and Anglo features which caused tourists and town folks to murmur when he and his father sold their chilies at the market. He sensed they wondered which of his parents was white, and which was the Indian, and when passing the old pueblo women sitting cross-legged on the plaza in Santa Fe, he'd close his eyes and turn away from their curious stares, eliminating, he thought, any evidence of his peculiar appearance.

He tried to stop the tears which snaked past his cheekbones to his mouth, but the salty taste caused his sorrow to deepen. He sobbed as memories of his father pulsed like neon lights within his mind. He recalled the stories Ojo related, usually late at night, the two of them alone behind the house. Ojo would pound the drum and talk of times before history existed, eons before his people received their name, "Te Tsu Geh." How their ancestor's spirits came into existence from the lake at Sandy Place, far to the north. They came from underneath the lake, Ojo would say, but not before they were cleansed with fire by older, wiser spirits which lived within the lake itself. Occasionally Ojo would lapse into Tewa, the ancient language of his people. Ben never understood his father when this happened, but Ojo's steady drum beats, which sometimes lasted until dawn, lingered in his soul.

He now felt emptied out like a dry arroyo in August since Ojo's sudden departure the week before, and wondered once more what caused his father to abandon them.

This morning was no different from any others since his father's disappearance. He stared across the small room at the bamboo fly rod Ojo had made for him, and Ojo's mud-caked boots poised at attention in the corner, then sadly recalled their early morning treks to the market. He glanced at the empty space above his bed where Ojo, a year ago, had nailed eagle feathers to the wall the night before his thirteenth birthday.

Ben heard his mother's slippers sliding down the hall, then closed his eyes and waited for Kate to say the same thing she'd said every morning since he could remember. "Ben, time to get up. You'll sleep your life away." He pulled the frayed blanket over his head and turned to face the mud wall. "It's time, Ben. It's Christmas Eve. We're walking to Chimayo."

He remembered all too well from years past the interminable procession with the neighbors to the tiny church beside the stream which usually froze during Christmas. He knew his hands and face would numb from the harsh wind they'd encounter on the back road which led them to the sanctuary. But his mother told them, "Baby Jesus was born in a cold, dark manger somewhere in the desert. You've got the chance to feel his pain, but you're lucky," she'd say, "you've got coats, he didn't, just a diaper." It was the same every Christmas Eve and while a sliver of moon still hung above the mountain, Ben rubbed his face and felt the sting of cold wood against his feet as he stepped onto the floor.

"Henry isn't dressed I bet," he mumbled, "and neither are you. Why do I have to go?"

"Your brother is ready, he's standing by the door."

"You and Henry go, I want to sleep."

"I'm counting to . . . ."

"I know, I know, but next year you're going without me."

"You sound just like your father. We'll be waiting on the porch."

For months Ben had felt the bitterness toward his parents grow. Initially he only resented the difference in their races which caused him to be shunned by natives and Anglos alike. But now he also blamed them for his impoverished condition and the harsh hand which fate had dealt him, so harsh, that to awaken each morning had become a struggle. And now he felt the pain of Ojo's absence on Christmas Eve.

The Touchstones were the first to cross the Taos highway and Ben was the last to fall in line behind Kate, who was leading the procession toward the river road. Soon they were joined by neighbors, their breaths streaming over their shoulders like steam from locomotives. When the pilgrims paused to wait for an elderly couple who lagged behind, Ben strained to locate the crows that cackled down at them, each outlined by the moonlight illuminating the road which wound down, then sharply up toward Chimayo.

Ben stared straight ahead at the stately figure of Kate, who carried herself with a dignified composure she'd earned from surviving hardships which others could only imagine. Ben knew what she'd endured, as did Henry, who chose to ignore it. Her imposing stature commanded respect and at that moment, she reminded Ben of a righteous piper leading them up to the promised land. The shawl, wound tight around her marble white neck, caused Kate to appear older than her fifty years. Ben saw her turn and flash those steel gray eyes, then signal for him to close the distance before the road bent and led higher toward the hills which encircled the isolated church.

She'd never said a word, but Ben was certain she sensed his mood. It was only after his father's unexpected departure the week before that this feeling of resentment had risen to the surface.

All around him Ben heard bits and pieces of 'Hail Marys' mumbled by the crowd, which now had swelled to over thirty, many he remembered from the day he entered grade school. Amelia Ocate, Kate's closest friend joined the group. Her thin, stooped figure draped in black, seemed too frail to withstand the trek to Chimayo.

His brother Henry turned to glare back, his straight onyx bangs framing dark eyes filled with contempt as he recalled what Ojo had often said to Kate: "Ben's going to be the one to make it in the white man's world. Ben's smart. With his good looks, he can pass for white any time, any place." Henry continued to glare until a scowl from Ben caused him to turn and huddle closer to Kate, who by now was sixty feet ahead.

Ben knew his mother shouldn't be walking to Chimayo. The doctor at the Indian clinic in Santa Fe had warned her not to overdo it, but Ben knew she wouldn't be deterred, especially when it came to her religion. His breath became harder to draw and he wondered how her heart was dealing with the steepness of the climb. He wasn't sure what the doctor had meant when he used the word 'congenital,' but sensed it wasn't good.

The pilgrim's mumblings had finally congealed. Their disconnected prayers and the "Pray for us sinners, now and at the hour of our deaths" was a unified chorus which filtered up between the black twisted branches that pointed the way to the church.

He saw his mother pause at the doors to the sanctuary, waiting with Henry who huddled by her skirt. Kate motioned for Ben to stuff his cap into his pocket before she fell to her knees to begin the slow crawl toward the altar, then finally into the cramped room which held the mysterious soil. Ben knew this was her intended destination and moving slowly behind Kate, he genuflected before the brightly painted tabernacle, then entered the small, dark chamber. He glanced up at the rows of crutches, holy cards and scribbled notes addressed to the Santo Niño in gratitude for miracles which had occurred after visits to the shrine. While Ben watched Kate kneel and reach into the hole to cross herself with the sacred dirt, he recalled the story of the Santo Niño's appearance and the cure of a cripple who'd crawled to the chapel a hundred years before. Kate moved slowly from the room toward the altar rail. Now it was Ben's turn. He reluctantly brought the soil to his forehead, over his heart and finally touched it to his shoulders.

The pungent smell of half-burnt votive candles mixed with incense stung his eyes. Alone, surrounded by fearsome shadows which danced across the walls, he blinked and stared up into the plaster eyes of the Niño above the hole. Suddenly, he felt a curious warmth surround him. He watched in disbelief as the mud walls suddenly began to pulse and shimmer, melting into what appeared to be liquid silver. Ben touched his face to see if he was dreaming. Stunned, he stared at the walls and ceiling which continued to ooze the glistening liquid. His breaths came in short gasps, then the fluid converged into a dazzling light which whipped into a circle above the statue. He smelled the scent of roses, then his jaw dropped and the strange warmth spread from his chest, through his arms and finally to his legs. Ben tugged at the buttons of his coat while the orb above the statue defined itself. He blinked again and rubbed his eyes, then suddenly the transparent figure of a delicate girl with exquisite features appeared and spoke in a soft, warm voice.

"Don't be frightened, Ben," she said softly. Her voice seemed to radiate from everywhere—the ceiling, the walls, even the dirt floor beneath his boots. "I'm your angel. The warmth you feel is love, Ben. It's the reason I exist, and the reason you exist."

He looked deep into her indigo eyes, the only color contained within her form which pulsed with the brilliance of the sun.

"I'm going to leave this feeling with you for awhile," she continued, as Ben's eyes widened. "What you do with it is up to you. Ben, you'll meet many people in your life. Some will be kind and thoughtful, but others will be dark, very dark, their souls filled with evil. You won't know the difference between them Ben, but they'll be there, and so will I. Now go to your mother. She's kneeling at the altar and needs your help."

He tried to swallow, but his dry tongue refused to move. His knees were weak, but the warmth produced a calmness he'd never experienced. Ben quietly left the room and found his mother kneeling alone, braced against the altar rail. She crossed herself, faltered and slumped toward the floor. It was at that moment she felt his arm around her waist, lifting her up toward the rail. She saw Ben smile and for the first time there was a kindness in his eyes she hadn't seen since he was very young.

"Come, mother, we'll sit together, you, me, and Henry. It's Christmas Eve. We're not alone tonight. We have each other." She felt his thin arm close tight around her waist and sensed his strength as he led her to the stiff wood bench.

Henry stared at Ben in disbelief. Disgusted, he looked away as Ben leaned to kiss his mother on the cheek as the solitary tone from the sacristy bell announced Mass was about to begin. Through the hour-long service, Ben stared up at the ancient carved reredos behind the altar, and suspended below, the chiseled figure of Christ twisted in pain, gaudily painted in the fashion of the Penitentes who had immigrated from Spain a hundred years before.

He continued to feel the strange warmth throughout Mass and became increasingly aware of the peaceful sensation he couldn't explain. Surely, he thought, it was caused by the closeness of the cluttered little room, or was it the votive candles depriving him of air? Possibly the strong incense had somehow affected his mind. But he knew he'd seen the girl and heard her voice. He tried to push it from his thoughts but her image and words persisted, even as they walked from the chapel, out into the cold night air.

"Children, it's time we go. They say we're due another storm today," murmured Kate as she dabbed her eyes and motioned for Henry to open the gate dividing the cemetery from the parking lot.

"It was a beautiful service, wasn't it?" asked Kate. Ben nodded in agreement. Henry said nothing and glared when Ben began to walk beside Kate as they moved slowly down the road toward Tesuque.

The wind stiffened from the north and beat against their overcoats, then Kate felt Ben's small, warm fingers gently squeeze her hand as the huddled trio began the wearisome journey home.

Several hours later, alone in the kitchen, Ben parted the pink dish towel Kate had hemmed into a curtain and stared into the blackness. Above his head, a bare light bulb hung from the ceiling which was woven from rough cedar logs and branches. He glanced down at the cracked formica counter which held a toaster, a stack of plastic plates and three open bowls filled with coffee, tea and sugar. A damp dish cloth draped the faucet above the small sink, stained brown by the brackish water from the well which served the pueblo. Shards of ice blew off the tin roof and past the window as Ben thought of where Ojo might be and what he was doing. He turned to face his brother.

"Henry, go back to sleep, it's late."

"It's Christmas, I can stay up all night if I want. Don't tell me what to do," said Henry in a sharp tone.

"I'm not telling you what to do."

"You do it all the time. You think you're better than . . . ."

"Better than you? Because you think I look more Anglo than you? That's been your problem all along, hasn't it?" replied Ben, his voice beginning to rise.

"No, it's just . . . ."

"I can't help the way I look, Henry. If I had a choice, I'd look like you, a full blood. You don't get gawked at. I know what they're thinking. Is his mother or father the Indian? I'm a freak. Don't you see, Henry? It's hard for me," shouted Ben, his face flushed with anger.

"The act you put on for mother at the church? Who do you think you're fooling? You never did anything like that before. Trying to get something extra in your stocking?"

"I wasn't acting. You'd never understand what happened in the room beside the altar," Ben said in a whisper. "It's late, I'm going to bed. Goodnight. Merry Christmas Henry," added Ben as he slid the towel across the window, switched off the light and made his way down the narrow hallway to his bed. Henry stood motionless in the kitchen and watched Ben close the door and his heart throbbed with jealousy and hatred which he nurtured toward his brother. Lately he'd relished it, even more now, because of what Ben had just confessed. He smiled, taking pleasure in knowing that Ben was troubled by the stares from the strangers. Henry repeated to himself the vow he'd made the year before: Someday he'd even the score between them—that Ben's good looks and Anglo features would somehow work against him. If not, he knew he was capable of making his brother suffer. Either way, he knew in time he'd bring his brother down.

In his room, Ben buried himself under the blanket and listened to the slabs of snow slide from the roof to the ground outside the window. He thought again of Ojo and wondered where he was, then, inexplicably, began to experience the warmth again, the same warmth he'd felt in the chamber at Chimayo. He closed his eyes and tried to recall the astonishing images: brilliant liquid silver which shimmered down the walls and the transparent, thin figure of the girl with the clearest, softest voice he'd ever heard. His heart slowed and filled with love which surged through his body. He said a prayer for Kate, another for Ojo, and one for Henry who was still standing in the kitchen, staring hard at the bedroom door.

At dawn the fragrance of fry bread summoned the two boys to the kitchen where Kate had hung nylon stockings above the sink. Henry rubbed sleep from his eyes. Ben yawned and settled at the table.

"I'm glad we went to Chimayo," said Ben gently.

"I thought you didn't want to, son? You said . . . ."

"I know, but after we got there, something happened."

"Happened?" asked Kate, "When I almost fell?"

"No, before that. I felt warm all over, then I saw an . . . ."

"Then you kissed mother on the cheek," snapped Henry who glanced at the chewing gum and the hard, red suckers nestled in the heels of the stockings.

"So?" asked Ben in a taut voice.

"Please boys, it's Christmas. Baby Jesus has come again. Let's be kind, especially today," said Kate over the rim of her coffee cup.

"Where do you think Ojo is?" questioned Ben, who lathered a slice of bread with jelly, then handed it to Henry.

"Don't know, probably never will," replied Kate before reaching for the nylons.

"Where are my eagle feathers?" Ben asked quietly. "Ojo gave them to me for my birthday. They were mine, now they're gone."

"I gave them away Ben."

"Why? They were special. Ojo said they'd give me strength."

"That's superstitious Ben. Eat your toast. I gave them to an old man I know who lives at Nambe Pueblo."

"What'll we do for money?" asked Henry as he slowly opened the candy Kate spread across the table. "Father isn't here to plant the chilies. The chile powder from last year's crop's almost gone." Then Henry shifted his attention to the unwrapped gum.

"I'll go to the market on Saturday and try to sell it," said Ben, his eyes fastened on the candy.

"Then what?" asked Henry. "Mother can't work. Her heart's not good, that's what the doctor said."

"We'll pray about it, boys. The Lord will work this out. He's never let us down," sighed Kate as she glanced at the piñon Christmas tree in the corner, its limbs dry and bent from lack of water.

"I'll go to work," offered Ben after a long pause.

"And do what?" asked Kate.

"Grow things. I can make anything grow, even flowers. Ojo taught me."

"The seeds can't be planted for several more months, Ben. Besides, you're still in school."

"I'll find work in town."

"In town?"

"In Santa Fe. Maybe work at someone's house on weekends, anything to bring in money."

"I'll speak to Father Ortiz tomorrow," said Kate as she wadded up the stockings and shoved them in the corner behind the toaster. "I wanted to speak to him after Mass last night, but we needed to start home. He's helped us out before. We'll see, but now we're going to have Christmas," added Kate, who glanced across the table at Henry, staring at the lifeless tree Ojo had cut the day before he vanished.

"Hail Mary full of grace, the Lord is with you," began Ben, his voice strengthening as Kate quietly joined the prayer. She glanced at Henry, his dark eyes fixed on Ben, the same dark stare of Ojo she'd seen countless times before.

That evening in the darkness, a candle quivered in its ruby colored holder, throwing long shadows of the Blessed Mother statue on the ceiling of the bedroom. Kate's head rested on the pillow as she glanced around the small room and studied the yellowed mantilla which crowned the Virgin's head, and the plain wood rosary dangling from the fingers of the statue. It was the rosary her mother had given her when she had been confirmed. A rusted heater purred in the corner, casting the same ruby color as the votive light beneath the statue. Her gray eyes blinked at the crucifix hanging by a mirror above the low wood chest. The statue rested on the chest, its plaster eyes staring back at Kate as she pulled the blanket to her shoulders.

Sleet, the size of mothballs, popped off the low, tin roof. Kate switched on the lamp, then brought the faded photograph of Ojo, Ben and Henry closer to her face. She had taken it when the boys were barely old enough to walk. She studied Ben's eyes which had a warmth about them, even at such a young age. Henry's eyes seemed different, more somber, with a distance to them she couldn't explain. She opened the medicine bottle, sipped from the glass and swallowed three pills the doctor had prescribed. Capping the bottle, she dipped her finger into the small, tin box filled with the mysterious soil from the chapel in Chimayo, rubbed it gently on her forehead and kissed the rosary beads twined between her fingers.

Years ago, Kate had stopped worrying about her health. She believed the Lord would take her when He was ready, not before. She glanced down at her swollen stomach, a mound under the worn, cotton blanket. Lack of exercise, she thought. Through the door, she heard Ben snoring. After several moments, Kate switched off the lamp, then closed her eyes.

Her dreams brought her back to childhood; to her mother Irene, kneeling by her bed to pray before she'd fall asleep. . . of sunny days in Hatch, on their farm picking chilies with her father. Next appeared his powdered face, lying in the casket when she was only twelve, and the aroma of the roses he gripped between his cold, rigid fingers. She saw her mother, kneeling by the grave after the priest had left the cemetery. At the end of the dream, Kate heard her mother's low, strong voice filter back: "He's in a better place, Kate. He's with God. Always keep your faith, dear, it's the only thing that's left, after all is said and done."

The year after her father died, Kate found her mother slumped across the kitchen floor. The doctor said later her heart had just stopped beating. Being the only child, Kate made the arrangements, and once more stood in the cemetery, this time alone, and recalled her mother's words from the year before: "Always keep your faith, dear, it's the only thing that's left, after all is said and done."

17

The following morning Kate sipped coffee by the window in the kitchen and watched Amelia walk slowly across the bridge toward the house. Amelia's small thin frame was bent and draped in black—black dress, black shoes, even the blouse she wore was black. Kate tried to recall if she'd ever seen Amelia wear anything but black, then waved at her friend as she approached while clutching a paper bag. Moments later Amelia entered and placed the bag on the small rectangular table, its legs sitting unevenly on the wood planked floor.

"What in the world? You didn't need to do this," said Kate in a forced manner.

"It's nothing, just a few things for Ben and Henry. I found them at the flea market. . . cost me next to nothing. Here, take them, I thought the boys could use them."

Amelia sighed as she sat and leaned against the table, then Kate asked softly, "You still miss Ruben, don't you Amelia?"

"Yes, even after burying him twenty years ago, I still see his face in my dreams. He was a kind man."

"I think of Ojo often, but after he left us the way he did," said Kate in a small voice which trailed off before Amelia asked, "You met in Hatch, didn't you?"

"Yes, I was working on our small farm. We only had ten acres. My father hired three men to help harvest the chilies. One of them was Ojo. He and I ended up working together. That's when I got to know him. You learn a lot about someone when you work bedside them twelve hours a day. Know what I mean?"

"Yes, Kate, I do. I met Ruben in Las Cruces. He pumped gas at a station across from the cafe where I waited tables. He came in every day and ordered the same thing. One thing led to another, then finally he proposed."

"Sounds like Ojo and me—but as you know, Ojo had a drinking problem. I thought I was destined to be the one to save him, but I was wrong. Maybe that's why I married him, thinking I could be his savior, to free him from himself. I was young then, and thought anything was possible. But that was a mistake, wasn't it Amelia? I mean thinking I could change him? I guess there was nothing I could have done. At first I was attracted by his kindness—and his looks. . . you know Ojo used to be quite handsome."

"I know," said Amelia through a sigh.

"But all that vanished after the liquor took hold of him," added Kate as she stared through the window at the pueblo, its peach colored houses blending with the hills.

Amelia nodded with understanding, then pulled out the sweaters and blue jeans from the bag and spread them on the table. "You think they'll fit?" she asked.

"Yes—yes they'll do nicely. Thank you. I don't know what I'd do without you," said Kate as she leaned to hug Amelia who turned toward the door.

Alone in the kitchen, Kate watched Amelia move across the bridge toward the pueblo. A brief thought of Ojo came and went as quickly as her heartbeat, then she turned to face the empty pantry, and her damp stockings hanging limp above the heater.

TWO

Luther Moquino closed his eyes and spread his long, thin arms to balance himself at the edge of the roof. He became an eagle, floating in the sapphire sky which stretched across the valley. One bare foot teetered on the ladder slanting from the roof to the dry, hard road which turned past his house, then ascended to the water tank, poised on a hill above the pueblo. He squinted at the letters scrawled across the tank, "Tesuque," and wished they'd used the ancient Tewa spelling, "Te Tsu Geh." His father, Leon, had told him what it meant: "Cottonwood Tree Place." He wasn't old enough to speak it well but Luther heard his parents and grandparents talk late into the evenings, sometimes using Tewa, their language handed down to them before time had been inscribed. The "Oral Tradition," they called it, the stories they'd leave for their descendants to cherish.

Luther appeared much older than fourteen: tall and lean, like his father, his black hair glistened and hung straight, almost to his slender waist. He had allowed no one to touch his hair with scissors since his tenth birthday. Leon said it gave him strength, the power he needed to face evil spirits which roamed the earth. His features mirrored Leon's—the gaunt face, high cheekbones and sunken eyes were the color of pecans he harvested in the autumn with his father.

A cat which blended with the dirt road stretched in the shadow of the roof. He watched it stir, then rub itself against the stiff, sun dried adobe bricks made from straw, mud and water which his ancestors had brought up from the river. Sweat worked down his face to the undershirt which needed to be washed. It was June, and Luther felt the need to plug himself back into the land, the trees, the rivers and the hot wind that whipped across his angular face.

He thought of Ben, who'd agreed to meet him in the cemetery beside the church at three o'clock, "Or maybe it was two?" he wondered aloud, then turned to face the cross of the church, and the bell beneath it, tethered in silence above the plaza of the pueblo. He watched for movement in the cemetery below, joined to the church by low adobe walls, then studied the weeds and wooden crosses leaning at odd angles above stones which marked the bodies of his loved ones.

Luther's deep-set eyes swept across the small, one story homes clustered around the plaza. All were built of adobe and appeared to him like cardboard boxes. He guessed the entire width and length of the pueblo would fit neatly within the boundaries of a football field. Some homes had smooth textured walls but others, especially the older ones which ringed the plaza, revealed their age—the adobe plaster had disintegrated, exposing round stones and small adobe bricks. Above the bricks, flat tarred roofs clutched round cedar beams which jutted out into the sunlight casting shadows on the bricks and stones. There were no straight lines to be seen within the structures, except for wood planks which framed the doors and windows. There was at once a hardness to the buildings and a warmth, derived from the pinkish, earthen color of adobe and the rounded edges shaped by human hands. Low, green juniper bushes and an occasional cottonwood flanked the hard dirt road which linked the dwellings, like a chain connecting rosary beads.

He heard a door slam, then saw his aunt, her arms heavy with clothes, walk slowly from her three room house toward a clothesline strung across the corner of the plaza.

Luther shielded his eyes from the glaring sun to study the four room adobe house across the river. Surrounded by a field of tall dry weeds, Ben's house reminded him of the older homes around the plaza, the difference being the tin roof, rusted from years of exposure to the elements which had also stripped the home of plaster to reveal rough adobe bricks. The front porch listed at a curious angle, which led his eyes to a torn screen loosely hinged over a broken window sealed with tape and cardboard. He shifted his attention back to the crosses and stones in the cemetery, then saw Ben crouched against the wall.

Luther made his way quickly down the ladder to the road and moments later pushed open the gate beside the church. Ben glanced in his direction, a dry weed stuck between his straight, white teeth.

"Where you been? inquired Ben as he shifted his attention to a mound of rocks covered by a board.

"On my roof, thinking," answered Luther who squatted next to Ben before he leaned against the wall.

"About?"

"About change. It seems things change too fast."

"Like what?" asked Ben who tossed the weed into the sand beneath his boots.

"Like all the signs they've stuck up on the highway. You can see them from my roof. And cars and trucks. Every night I hear them on the road. Used to be, I could go to sleep and hear the river and the birds, and the sound of wind coming down the mountain. No more Ben. All I hear are trucks."

"I know what you mean. I'm even closer to the road, it's worse for me. So what d'ya think, Luther?"

"I'd like to go back to when I was a little boy. Leon used to take me fishing on the Pecos. Wouldn't see another person for hours. Now it's elbow to elbow. Barely room to cast a caddis fly."

"Yeah, I know," said Ben who frowned, spit, then picked another weed.

"Wouldn't it be wonderful to have lived a hundred years ago?" asked Luther, his mahogany eyes fixed on some faded plastic flowers resting in the sand above a grave.

"Yeah, but we've got to go on. You can't sit around and think of the past. There's plenty to look forward to."

"What?" asked Luther in a low voice while he focused on a wooden cross.

"Finishing school, getting a job and make some money. Then I could take better care of mother and Henry. Maybe build another house, a bigger one for us to live in."

"You think that will make you happy?"

"No, not just that. There's other things."

"Such as?"

"The good feeling of helping others who have bigger problems than my own. I've had talks with the old priest in Chimayo. He said to trust God, and think of other people."

"That sounds too simple, Ben. Don't you feel trapped inside this place? I think most Anglos don't want us to get ahead. They think we're useless."

22

"Not all Anglos feel that way. A lot do, but I've met some who aren't like that. But I haven't been around them all that much."

"I have, when I worked at Kaune's last summer in Santa Fe bagging groceries. Some treat you like, like. . . ."

"Second class people?" said Ben before Luther could finish.

"Yeah, or worse."

"Worse?"

"Ignore you," answered Luther in a distant tone.

"People like that don't treat anyone with respect, even their own family and friends."

"Yes, I suppose. But I still feel trapped," said Luther as he shifted his back against the hard adobe wall.

"So, Luther. . . what d'ya gonna do?"

"Clay."

"Clay?"

"Make pots, like grandad used to do. I hear they sell for big bucks in Santa Fe. Big bucks."

"Ever done it?"

"Once. Grandad took me to a room behind his house where he worked clay with his hands then put it in an oven, a big oven. Later they came out black, black as ink. He'd sign them on the bottom then take them into town. Mother says his pots sell for more money than you can count. I tried it that afternoon. It felt good, the wet dirt between my fingers."

A hush crept between the two boys who both stared at the broken crosses, thinking about what each had said. Luther pictured his grandfather, bent over the wheel, spinning magic from his wrinkled hands. Then Ben thought of Kate and if she needed help with dinner.

"I hear there's rainbow trout rising in the river at Cundiyo," said Luther after a long pause. "Even German browns, big ones," he quickly added.

"Yeah?" said Ben in an upturned voice.

"How about a trip? We can fish the top of the canyon to the bottom. Spend the weekend camping out," said Luther while glancing at the sun above the church.

"You got camping stuff?" asked Ben.

"I can borrow some from Uncle Arthur. All you'll need is fishing gear."

"Ojo left the rod he made for me. It's beautiful, split bamboo. And his fly reel. Guess he didn't need it. Do you ever see him in the pueblo? Is he living there?"

"Yeah," answered Luther as he stood, brushed off his jeans and turned to face Ben still crouched against the wall. "I heard he's got a day job at Embudo taking tourists down the Rio Grande. He comes back late, I hardly ever see him."

"Does he live alone?" asked Ben in a small voice.

"He's taken up with a Tesuque girl half his age. He's old enough to be her father."

Ben's eyes dropped to the parched sand between his legs. He closed his eyes, and felt his heart sink to the bottom of his stomach. Stunned, he felt sickened from the image of his father, holding someone in his arms besides Kate. "Let's go fishing," Ben said quietly.

"I'll get what we need and pick you up Friday morning at sunrise. Leon works weekends in Truchas. He can take the high road and drop us at the canyon. Bring a poncho and a blanket. We can probably count on rain," said Luther as he made his way past the gate and up the dust filled road toward his house.

Three days later Ben heard the tires in the gravel drive, then through the fog, saw the glare of taillights as the truck slowed beside the gate.

"Does Kate know you're going?" asked Luther as Ben approached in the darkness. Luther clutched the small, leather medicine bag between his fingers as Ben greeted Leon, then swung himself over the tailgate and settled in the back of the truck beside Luther.

"Of course she knows," replied Ben. "I'd never leave without telling her. Amelia Ocate is staying while I'm gone."

"What's wrong with Henry? He's been acting weird," asked Luther who steadied himself as the truck lurched toward the highway.

"He's worse than ever. Don't trust him. Sometimes he leaves early, doesn't come home 'till late at night. No, it's better if her friend is there. I won't worry." Ben thought for a moment before asking Luther in a cautious voice, "What's in your medicine bag?"

"Be patient, Ben. Someday, I might give it to you."

The thin air felt cool against their skin as Leon shifted gears, then glanced in the mirror at the boys. Red glass rosary beads swayed beneath the mirror as the truck struggled higher through the mountains. Ben stared down at the valley and watched the lights of the pueblo grow dim from the sunlight which swept away the fog.

"You asleep?" asked Ben, who glanced at Luther, facing forward, his back propped against the rusted tailgate.

"No, just thinking of my dream."

"What dream?" asked Ben.

"Last light I dreamed I was floating over the mountain. I looked to the west and saw the moon, which was red, red as blood. Then big waters came down from the mountains and filled the rivers, and soon they flooded the pueblo. Even the bell of the church was underwater. I saw the spirits of my family, even my ancestors, resting on the surface. Then other spirits, trapped beneath, struggled to the top. But the Great Spirit kept them down, as if they weren't ready for the journey. Finally, after a long time, the Great Spirit allowed them to join the others."

"What's it mean?"

"Don't know. It must mean something. I'll ask Leon. He says good spirits bring us dreams, bad ones bring us terror."

"Do you believe that?"

"Yes, every word," answered Luther who yawned and slouched against the pack.

The truck turned sharply then straightened over the plateau which loomed above Chimayo. Ben watched the sun expose fractures in the peach colored hills as he glimpsed the tower of the church. He thought of the angel and wondered if she'd ever come again. "Do your spirits have faces?" Ben asked.

Luther stirred, then steadied himself as Leon shifted gears. "Yes, I see them in my dreams."

"You talk so freely about spirits. We Catholics don't. Even Kate. She keeps things like that to herself."

"They're part of us Ben. They fill the stories handed down to us. The stories tell us where we came from and where we're headed. It's all connected: rivers, fire, the sun, trees and animals. All things have souls. Everything's woven together like threads in a tribal blanket. It's about how we care for each other and show respect for the gifts God has given us. That's the difference between us and Anglos. They've got it backwards. Anglos think they own the earth. They believe man should be in control, to do whatever he likes with the environment. We believe all things are gifts from God. That's why things are so screwed up. In the end, the Great Spirit will prevail. Do your spirits have faces?" asked Luther as he turned to face the wind, his long, black hair streaming backward.

"Only one I know of. I saw her in the church at Chimayo last Christmas. She was young and beautiful. Her eyes were blue, but I could see right through them. Then she disappeared."

"Was this a dream?" Luther asked cautiously as he zipped the windbreaker closer to his neck.

"I don't think so. I could smell the candles while she talked. Then she left me with this feeling."

At Cundiyo, the truck veered off the highway onto a steep road which twisted deep into the canyon. They descended further, past a filling station, and an old woman who waved from a isolated shack, perched on a ledge above the river. Cool spray rose from the canyon, sending mist across the road. Suddenly the boys heard the roar before they saw the water surge under the bridge, then Leon abruptly stopped the truck. Far below, the river crashed against the boulders and rumbled through the canyon like thunder. Ben cinched his pack tight against his shoulders and watched Luther wave to Leon, who was halfway up the road leading from the canyon.

"No way we can fish here. Too rough. We'll hike down," said Luther as he studied the swirling water, a hundred feet below. He chose the high trail, which followed the river as it wound down through the belly of the mountain. An hour later they descended to a sandbar below a pool, where the river made a wide, slow turn.

"Try a caddis fly, Ben. Tie enough tippet on, these trout are leader shy," said Luther as he pointed to small, white insects lifting off the water like tiny bits of cotton.

Luther watched Ben grasp the fly. The delicate, light colored wings, fashioned from elk hair, stood upright on its body which he held between his fingers. Ben carefully slipped the tippet through the eyelet, then looped it several times around itself and clenched the knot. Soon they were casting, rods bending back and forth in rhythm, slinging great loops of line which sliced the air above their heads. Ben pointed to a red-tailed hawk drawing circles in the clouds, then watched it swoop toward the river, wings pinned against its body as it streaked low across the water.

Ben felt a peacefulness from the sound of water curling over stones. The heavy scent of pine and spruce filled his senses, then suddenly, he saw the huge fish rise toward the fly and in a flash, snatch it from the surface. Startled, Ben hesitated, then raised the rod and felt the power of the fish. Line ripped past the rod tip. He raised it once again and tried to halt the line from screaming off the reel. The bamboo rod bent further and further. Suddenly, the trout burst from the water, twisting in midair to free itself from the predator. Ben's heart raced as he staggered over the rocks toward the fish which plunged to deeper current. He quickly eased pressure on the line, while his prey continued to run in long, slow arcs. It leapt again, as if to demonstrate its majesty. Ben stumbled to his knees. The line ripped past his fingers, then the current swept the fish to deeper water.

Luther dropped his rod and ran across the sandbar. Carefully, Ben began to turn the fish upstream, guiding it in slow, wide circles toward the bank. Now on its side, breathing hard against the gravel, he saw its black eyes staring back in resignation. He knew he'd caught a record setting trout. Now it was his decision—not Luther's, not Kate's, not Ojo's, but his alone, and his heart quickened as he knelt beside the fish.

He grasped it by the belly. Luther stood quietly beside him. He felt for the hook, deep inside its mouth. His fingers worked quickly. He knew in several more seconds the trout would die. He paused for a moment and glanced at Luther. He saw it twitch, then undulate, its fins moving in the air with slow, short strokes. Suddenly, Ben felt the warmth again. He couldn't explain it, nor would he be able to explain it later to Luther, Kate, or anybody else. It was a mystery. Finally he freed the hook. Moving to deeper water he gently turned the trout upstream, then opened his fingers and watched it swim slowly through the shallows to the middle of the river.

That evening, beside the campfire, Luther sat cross-legged and watched smoke rise toward the moon. Ben sat across from him in silence and thought about what had happened on the river.

"That was good Ben, what you did today. I didn't think you'd let him go."

"Surprised myself, Luther. I got this feeling when I stooped to take the hook out. Like something told me what was best to do."

"Does your angel still come to you?"

"No. Haven't seen her since Christmas Eve."

"You didn't see her today, but maybe she came to you beside the river."

"Don't know Luther, but something happened inside me. I rarely let a trout go, especially one that big."

"Wait, Ben. . . do you hear it?"

"Hear what?"

"The wind on the water, moving down the canyon."

"Yes. And I feel it too, I'm putting on my sweater."

"Ben. Listen. It's the spirits. They're pleased with you Ben, I can feel it. There's a closeness with nature you've never had before."

"Maybe," said Ben in a weary voice before he stoked the fire and pulled the tribal blanket closer to his face.

Luther sat alone in thought. He lit the smudge stick, a thin bundle of dried sage and cedar, and brushed the smoke across his face, then past his ears to purify himself before he slept. He studied the universe whirling in the sky above the campfire. A wolf's cry echoed down the canyon. Suddenly, a branch snapped. Luther turned and saw yellow eyes glowing back in the darkness. The fire popped and sent embers up to paradise, which Luther knew was somewhere out in space. He felt the world was right, and maybe after all, he shared the angels with his friend, curled up by the fire, asleep.

At dawn, cool drizzle descended on the canyon from low, gray clouds, which woke the boys tucked inside their blankets. Ben rose first and tried to light the fire. Luther lay quietly under his poncho and listened to the raindrops muffled by tall pines which swayed above the campsite.

"Have some fry bread," Ben mumbled through the rain which had formed a pool beside his blanket. He gazed across the river at cottonwoods lining the bank, their saffron colored leaves stirred by wind which softened to a murmur. He looked further downstream as it narrowed to a ribbon beneath the ridge which pierced the drab, gray sky.

"Let's move down," Ben said after Luther finished eating. "There's a long run of riffles, then a pool which might be full of trout." Luther nodded then stuffed the blanket and clothes into the backpack.

They struggled higher up the rocks toward the trail. Ben led the way as the rush of water became a whisper. An hour passed before they left the trail and descended to the river with the packs drawn tight against their shoulders.

Ben was first to wet a caddis fly. Luther moved just below him, casting to the middle of the pool.

"Ben?"

"Yes?"

"My dad wants me home early."

"Today?"

"Yeah. Said they're planning something for my mother's birthday. He's picking us up later today, at the bridge where he left us."

Ben halted his cast and turned to Luther who was stripping in line as it drifted with the current. "I really looked forward to another night of camping," Ben said with disappointment, as Luther flexed the rod, then shot sixty feet of line across the pool.

"Nothing I can do. He'll be at the bridge at four. I've got to go."

Ben fell silent and resumed casting, moving the rod back and forth in rhythmic arcs. On the third cast, he released the line and watched it loop gracefully in the air. The caddis fly landed softly, its wings erect as it floated with the current.

"I think I'll stay the night, Luther. Go meet your dad. Kate doesn't expect me 'till tomorrow, but let her know I'm staying," said Ben as he stripped in line and waited for a strike.

"Where will you camp?" asked Luther as he mended the line across the slow moving current.

"Don't know. The clouds are moving out. I'll be fine."

"We'll pick you up tomorrow. Meet us at the bridge at noon."

For several hours they continued to fish the pool, then moved further up to faster water. At two, Luther packed his rod and reel then waved at Ben from the narrow trail, high above the river.

Alone, Ben worked his way upstream and fished until the moon emerged, a sliver of a fingernail above the ridge. He made camp close beside the water to hear it dance across the stones.

During the night beside the fire, Ben rested on his pack and studied the stars which seemed like jewels thrown across a blanket. He thought of Luther. Luther was right. He did feel closer to the earth. In a way he envied Luther, taking all there was in nature to the center of his soul. He closed his eyes and thanked God for all He had given.

At dawn he woke to the rumble. It seemed distant, further up the river. Suddenly, a fierce crack of lightning spilt the sky. Stunned, he covered his face with his hands. It struck again, much closer, then thunder filled the canyon. Deafened by the roar, he reached for the pack, but it had vanished. In horror, he stared as the water rushed toward him, a wall of roiling foam which came from nowhere. Another shock of lightning split the tree above his head. Dazed, he struggled to his feet, then suddenly his legs gave way to the force which pulled him from the bank. He fought against its strength—his thin arms flailed at waves which crashed above his head and sucked him under. His shirt ripped from his chest. Swept by the surge, stones lashed his skin. Ben cried out as his body slammed against a boulder, then blood filled his mouth. Exhausted, he fought against the power, but was pulled beneath the swell. His life rushed past: a flash of Kate in the kitchen, another of Ojo with his knife against his mother's throat, then Henry glaring back at him. He gasped for air and prayed he wouldn't die, not here, not alone in a canyon by himself. His head struck something hard, then pain shot through his skull.

Suddenly, he felt something seize his arm, far stronger than the water which pinned him to the rocks. Wrenched from the bottom, something seemed to lift him from the flood. It was then he sensed the strong, broad shoulders which carried him toward the shore. Sprawled across the sandbar, he stared up at long, white hair dripping water on his chest, then saw the wrinkled face and soft, gray eyes. "You were almost gone, boy. My name's Two Crows. I saw you from the ridge going under and knew you wouldn't last."

Ben touched the blood smeared across his face and arms. He breathed deeply, then tried to stand, but the pain drove him to the ground.

"Be still boy. You're hurt. Catch your breath, then I'll carry you up to my place."

Ben ached from the bruises and the cuts which bled into the sand. Several minutes passed before he stood and leaned across the shoulders of the old man, who bent, then grasped his arms and legs.

"Hold on. We've got quite a climb. It won't be long, just lay still across my shoulders." They ascended slowly, then left the trail and rested briefly beneath a stand of aspens. "A bit further and we're there. I'll bandage you up, feed you, then you need to sleep. You'll be fine boy, don't worry, Two Crows will take care of you." Then he stooped again and hoisted Ben across his shoulders.

At midnight Ben woke and blinked at the stars above his head through the smoke flaps of a tepee. He studied the round, gray stones which circled the fire in the center, throwing shadows against the canvas walls, painted white. The figure of a bison, painted red, stretched from the ground toward the tall, wood poles which met above the smoke flaps. He breathed in sage and cedar, and thought of Luther's smudge stick. Nearby, a propane stove rested on a low, wood table. Another sleeping bag, which was empty, lay crumpled by the entrance.

Ben stared down at the bandages on his chest and arms. The old man had been gentle, he remembered, dabbing soap and water on his wounds. He was grateful for the meal and especially for the dry clothes which seemed to fit. He fell asleep thinking of Two Crows and how he'd risked his life to save a stranger.

At dawn, light slanted through the doorway of the tepee. A single plume of smoke spiraled up the canvas walls, then out through the flaps above his head. He rubbed his eyes and saw a small, clay pipe resting on the table, and beside it, a pouch filled with dark colored tobacco.

Ben stood and listened. Silence. Nothing moved except the fire which sputtered back to life. At that moment, he saw something glimmer by the fire pit. He knelt, then brought the chain closer to his face. The silver cross was scarred, the edges smooth from wear. A mound of orange coral was fixed in the center. A crow's foot was stamped into the back.

"Two Crows? Are you here? It's Ben, you saved my life," shouted Ben from inside the tepee. He stood motionless and waited for an answer. He dropped the chain beside the fire pit, then ducked through the entrance, out into the strong, clear light. He scanned the ridge for any sign of movement. Then he saw the meadow fifty feet away bursting with flowers, and further down, a stand of aspens. He called out, but was answered by his own voice which tumbled down the canyon.

By the angle of the sun, Ben knew he had little time to waste. He recalled that Luther said they'd meet him at the bridge at noon. If he was late, they'd form a group and start to search. Kate would be called and she would worry.

The sunlight warmed his back as he made his way through the meadow to the trail which ended at the tepee. He felt secure. He'd hiked up the canyon several times before, though never this far. For two hours he descended and thought of Two Crows. Who was he? And why he'd left him alone in the tepee? Probably fishing, Ben assumed, or hunting for his dinner.

First he saw Luther wave from the river, his rod flexed as he cast across the current. Then he saw the truck, and Leon sitting on the tailgate eating lunch. Ben made his way toward the bridge and waited as Luther approached, his rod slung across his shoulder.

"Good God Ben! What's happened?" he shouted, then motioned for Leon to join him at the bridge.

Ben stopped. The bandage on his head had unraveled and trailed to the ground. Luther stared back as if Ben was an apparition, a ghost from somewhere in the canyon, then Luther saw the blood stains on his shirt.

"What the hell?"

"A storm came up," Ben said quietly as he glanced at Luther, then at Leon. Both stood motionless and stared at Ben.

"A wall of water swept me off the bank. Then I fell into the river."

"Who bandaged you? Where did you get those clothes?" asked Luther who moved closer.

"All I know is, I was at the bottom of the river. I felt something pull me up. Then an old, white-haired man named Two Crows, carried me ashore. He lifted me on his shoulders, then took me to his tepee, high up in the canyon above the timberline. He bandaged my cuts, fed me, then I fell asleep. When I woke this morning he was gone. Then I followed the trail back to the bridge."

Luther shot a long, questioning glance at Leon, then paused before he said, "We'd heard about a storm above Truchas. But nothing like this. You lost your rod and reel?"

"Yes, and almost lost my life," said Ben in a hushed tone as he limped toward the truck.

An hour later he was home. Kate heard the door slam. She dropped her rosary and saw him standing in the kitchen, cuts and bruises on his face and arms. She stood and walked toward him, when he said in a tired voice, "Had a problem in the canyon, but I'm all right. I need some sleep. We'll talk later."

Kate remained silent as Ben walked past her to his room. She was grateful he was back, unharmed and safe within their home. Kate knew eventually he would tell her what had happened. He was good about such things, never holding back the truth.

Ben stared at the vigas in the ceiling. He heard the wind sweep down the mountain where he'd almost lost his life and pulled the blanket closer to his face. His mind reached back to Luther's dream—of rivers which filled the valley and covered the pueblo. Was Luther's dream a vision? he wondered.

He would never tell Kate what had happened. He knew she would worry if he ever went again. No, he thought, he would keep it to himself, but Two Crows would wander through his mind for many years to come.

A week passed and Kate continued to hide the ache which simmered in her heart. She knew Ojo was with another woman, a pueblo girl she'd heard, and unlike her, young and healthy. She wasn't certain now how long he'd stay away, but his drinking had almost cost her life. She recalled the night a year before when Ojo returned from what he claimed was a meeting with the Governor of the Pueblo. He quietly entered their bedroom. Kate remembered she'd awakened when she smelled the perfume as he stumbled into bed.

She regretted confronting Ojo. She knew now she should have remained silent until his shallow breathing became a snore. She ought to have waited until morning.

She had shook him, then demanded to know the woman's name. She recalled the knife was shaking as he held it to her throat. She remembered the touch of cold steel pressed against her skin, and the dark look in Ojo's eyes before he made the threat. "If you say a word about her, I will kill you," Ojo slurred, "then skin you like a deer."

Kate sighed as she stared out the window at Ben kneeling in the garden, hunched over the thin, straight rows he'd dug that morning. She watched his small fingers gently drop the chile seeds, one by one into the furrows, as if each one had its own identity. Ben considered them pearls, but she thought of them as only seeds. Kate watched him for over an hour, smiling, bent over the hard cracked soil enclosed by the wire fence which needed mending.

The clouds resting on the mountain thickened into amber colored pillows. Ben continued to plant his garden, each seed placed with care within the furrows. While he worked, Ben recalled images of the angel. He felt the warmth in a corner of his heart—she'd given just enough for him to face another day. He wanted her to come again, to see her face glow gently and hear her words which gave him hope. He thought of his longing to see her as he dropped another seed on the crusted earth beneath his boots.

Suddenly, the breeze shifted and brought the smell of whiskey which he'd come to dread. Then a shadow fell across the furrows. Ben stiffened when he heard his father's hard-edged voice.

"It's me Ben, I've come to get you." Ben swallowed hard and turned slowly, then looked up into Ojo's dark, bloodshot eyes.

"Why'd you come back? You left us when we needed you most. You don't love us. If you did, you never would have left."

"Shut your mouth. You're not old enough to understand," shot back Ojo.

"I'll never be old enough to understand. What you've done is wrong. Mama needed you—still does, but we'll make out, you'll see."

"You want to know where I'm staying?"

"No, don't tell me. It makes me sick to think of you with someone else. Besides, it's wrong. You're married. You're supposed to be with mama, not another woman. God knows what you've done."

"Got religion now, do you? Kate's been filling your head with ideas about God, has she? Or maybe it's her friend, the old priest up in Chimayo?"

"No, it's neither of them. I just know what's right and what's wrong. Nothing you can say will change it."

Ojo wiped sweat from his tanned, leathery face, then coughed and staggered backward, his eyes enraged. His fingers squeezed into fists as he turned to see Kate at the kitchen window staring back in silence.

"You're coming with me son. Drop the seeds and get in the truck. Do it now," he slurred before steadying himself against the fence post.

"No Ojo. When you left that night, you left forever. You haven't been here to hear mama crying in her sleep or see her barely move from the kitchen to her bed. Her heart's not good, and getting worse. You knew that when you left. Your drinking almost killed her."

"What d'ya mean?"

"You know what I mean. The night you came in drunk and put your knife to her throat. I saw you through the bedroom door," declared Ben in short, quick gasps.

"You've got some strange ideas in your head. You talk like a white boy."

"You always said I could pass for one. Aren't you pleased?"

"You're my son and I'm coming back for you and Henry when it's time. You won't know when, but I'll be back. You're going to grow up in the pueblo where you belong, around people who are your own kind. Even if I've got to force you. Tell that to Kate and Henry—that I'll be back."

Ben's eyes followed Ojo as he staggered to the truck. Then Ben heard him curse as he shifted gears and drove wildly down the road toward the river. Tears coursed down Ben's face and fell to the soil between his knees. Then a finger touched his shoulder. He looked up at Kate, who was rigid, cold, almost lifeless.

"He said he's coming back. Said he'd take me and Henry. I'm afraid. I won't go, no matter what he does to me."

"Don't be worried son. When he returns, we'll face him. You and me together."

"And God, mother. He'll be with us, just like always. Nothing will hurt us, my angel told me so."

"Your angel?" said Kate with surprise.

"Yes, she came to me in Chimayo on Christmas Eve. Right before you almost fell at the altar rail, then I caught you and led you to the pew?"

"Yes, I remember. You had the kindest look about you. . . but I'm making supper. I'll call you when it's done."

An hour passed while Kate slapped dough into thin, white circles. She thought of Henry, and wondered where he was. His absence reminded her of Ojo as she called out to Ben, still hunched over the rows of dirt.

Ben pulled his chair closer to the table, then stared at the plate of refried beans and empanadas before he asked timidly, "Who does Ojo live with?"

Kate looked away. "With someone else, across the river in the pueblo," she answered with a sigh.

"I thought so. It's wrong. I told him so."

"He wanted another woman, Ben, someone young and healthy. Don't you remember what the doctor said? I've got heart problems. I'm getting older."

"I don't care. If he loves you, none of that would matter. Did he ever love you?"

"At first he did, years ago, but when the doctor. . . ."

"You mean when the doctor said your heart was bad—that's when he left?" asked Ben.

"Yes, that's when he left."

"But that's when you needed him most. He should have stayed. I don't understand."

"It's a long story, Ben. I'll explain it when you're older. Now eat your dinner and go to bed."

Ben glanced at his plate and the mound of refried beans he'd barely touched, then asked, "Why did you marry him in the first place?"

"When we first met, he was a kind and gentle man. Always thinking of others. When we were in the fields picking chilies, he'd always lend a hand if someone needed help. I remember one day, the year before you were born, when another worker fell sick. Ojo did the work of two men that day, but never told my father. On Friday, the man collected his full paycheck, as

35

if nothing had happened. Ojo was like that years ago. Back then, Ojo was a handsome man. Clear, proud eyes. . . his body was firm and lean, but then he started drinking more and more. It changed him, Ben, into someone I hardly recognized. I thought I could save him from it—and I tried, believe me I tried, but there was nothing I could do."

Ben fell silent while he picked at his food, then said goodnight and wandered off to bed. Curled in a ball under the covers, he struggled in the darkness, tormented with thoughts, searching through the night for peace. He studied the slice of moon through the window and wondered whether he should love or hate his father. Finally, he closed his eyes and fell asleep.

At sunrise, low, dark clouds gathered in the hills above the river. A truck crossed the bridge and drove slowly up the drive. A dog barked. Ben stirred beneath the sheet. A door slammed, then a loud noise in the kitchen brought him to his feet.

He heard voices, then Kate screamed. He rushed into the kitchen and saw Ojo standing in the doorway, a bottle clutched between his fingers. Sweat coursed down Ojo's face, consumed in rage. Long black hair hung in strings across his eyes. Then he slammed the door. The windows shook. Ben moved closer to Kate who screamed again when Ojo smashed the bottle on the counter. He staggered toward them and held the pointed shards of glass against her stomach.

"He's coming with me. I've got Henry in the truck," Ojo slurred. Kate and Ben backed into the corner of the cramped room, now filled with the stench of urine on his clothes and liquor on his breath. His nostrils flared and his hands trembled. Then Ojo slowly raised the bottle and pressed it to her neck. Kate began to breathe in short, quick gasps as Ojo wiped saliva from his swollen lips. As Ben lunged toward him, Ojo spotted his wounds, pink slits of skin, puckered at the edges.

"You been beating him Kate? Or was it the Chimayo priest? They whip themselves up there in Chimayo. Is that who did it?"

Kate sobbed, shook her head then pulled Ben closer to her waist.

"No," shouted Ben. "Stop it." The bottle crashed to the floor. Ojo seized Ben's arms. "It hurts, stop it!" Ben screamed as Ojo dragged him out the door and down the steps toward the truck. The headlights glared at Kate who braced herself against the railing, her hands clutched against her chest.

Ojo pushed him inside. Then in the mirror, Ben saw Henry curled against the tailgate. The engine roared. Suddenly, Kate slumped and fell against the railing. Ojo's massive hands gripped Ben's arm as he struggled to open the door.

"Mama's dying!" Ben screamed. "Can't you see?"

At that moment, Ojo felt a cold steel barrel press against his skull. Then he heard the lever snap a shell into the chamber. He froze.

"Shut off the engine, Ojo." Ben stared at the rifle shoved through the open window.

Ojo reached for the keys.

"Slowly, I want to see your hands." Then silence. Henry moved closer to the tailgate and covered his eyes. Ben strained in the low light to see the face, then saw a finger curl around the trigger.

"Ben, take Kate and Henry inside and lock the door," whispered the low voice. Ojo sat motionless. The barrel remained fixed, pointed at his brain. His bloodshot eyes tracked Ben as he helped Kate through the doorway, followed by Henry who quickly locked the door.

"Ojo, you're an animal, no, less than an animal. If I ever see you here again, I'll blow your head off. Any questions?" Ojo shook his head, then cautiously turned the key.

Moments later, Luther Moquino turned toward the house to conceal his face as Ojo backed slowly down the driveway. Ojo glared at the figure standing on the porch. He knew he would return, but next time with his shotgun—and maybe kill them all.

Luther watched the taillights fade to a dull glow, then heard the gate close behind the house. He neared the garden and saw Ben crouched in the furrows, his head between his knees.

"Ben? Are you O.K.?"

Ben straightened, turned, then saw Luther standing by the fence.

"What are you doing here?"

Luther said nothing. Then Ben saw the rifle propped against the gate.

"That was you?"

"Yes."

"How did you. . . ."

"Know to come?" asked Luther in a somber tone.

Ben nodded. Luther moved closer.

"Luther, it was horrible. Ojo almost murdered mother. He held a broken bottle to her throat. I tried to stop him, then he drug me out and threw me in the truck. Made me sick to my stomach. That's why I came outside."

"How is Kate?"

"She's calmed down a little. She's in her room."

"Did she tell you I was by earlier?" asked Luther as he glanced back toward the driveway.

"No."

"I had a dream. I came by to tell you about it. I dreamed I was walking in the river by the pueblo, but it was dry, dry as cow's bones. The moon was huge, the color of butter. In the darkness I saw everything around me, even birds sleeping in the cottonwoods. A wolf howled, high on the hill above the pueblo. Another wolf, with cubs huddled by her side, answered with a cry. They were very close, I could almost touch them. I watched the first one move down to the arroyo. The willows parted. Its eyes were red like blood as it studied the others next to me—there were three of them, the mother and her cubs. She stood and growled as he approached. His teeth sparkled in the moonlight. She growled again, but deeper, then he lunged. She fought as best she could, but he shredded her to pieces. Then he dragged the cubs into the arroyo and killed them with his teeth."

Luther paused, then glanced at Ben staring at the rows of dirt between his feet.

"Will Ojo come back?" asked Ben with apprehension.

"Don't know. He was drunk, real drunk. He won't remember half of what he did. Keep my rifle, you may need it," said Luther as he turned and walked toward the driveway and disappeared around the corner of the house.

Ben saw Kate through the window, sitting on the bed, her head buried in her hands. He felt a breeze against his face, then watched a large, yellow moon sink behind the hill.

"Ben, get Henry. He's playing in back behind the garden," snapped Kate while she waited in the hot, dry sun beside the porch.

"Henry doesn't want to go," shouted Ben from the doorway.

"Tell him to get outside this minute. He'll be sorry if he makes us late," Kate replied in a sharp voice as she stared at the one lane road leading to the highway.

They moved down the drive in single file, with Henry at the rear throwing rocks at cowbirds balanced on the fence.

"Come along boys. We can't be late."

"How many will be there?" asked Ben as he shielded his eyes from the sun which burned away the morning clouds.

"I don't know Ben. They said to be there at eleven. They're waiting for us."

The road continued east, but the group veered left on a small gravel path, the center of it filled with weeds. The sun bore down on Kate and the boys. Even Henry, who was eleven, struggled with the heat.

"Have they locked him up?" asked Ben who motioned for Henry to close the gap between them.

"They said for us to come, that's all I know," sighed Kate as she frowned into the sun.

The path dipped into an arroyo, its tan, cracked clay sprouting cedar and chamisa. Sweat stained the blouse she'd ironed the night before, but Kate moved with courage. Then her stride lengthened as she led them higher through the hills.

They stopped at the ridge and saw the small metal building with the pueblo flag popping in the wind above the roof.

"See the cars and trucks. We're late," said Kate as she waited for Henry who stopped to urinate on the weeds between his feet.

They knocked and heard the sound of chairs scrape against the floor. Slowly, they entered the one room office. Twelve men stared back in silence. The air was close and filled with smoke. A fan swiveled on a table in the corner. Kate glanced at Arthur Mora, the Governor of the Pueblo.

"Sit down Kate. Boys, sit beside your mother." Mora lit a cigarette and stared at Kate, her face lowered to the floor.

Several of the men cleared their throats and waited. In the corner, the fan continued to purr. Ben looked sideways at Henry. Kate raised her head and studied Mora's face, tanned and lined from the farm he tended by the river. She'd seen him every spring, tilling, planting then harvesting in the autumn. She also knew his wife, but they hardly ever spoke.

"Kate?"

"Yes?" she said in a composed manner as Ben leaned forward, his hands tucked between his knees.

"The council met last night, including Gilbert Zuniga, chief of tribal police. Everyone who was at the meeting, is sitting here now," said Mora in a solemn tone.

Kate nodded calmly.

"We've all known Ojo for a long time. We know he has a drinking problem, a bad one. We also know the other night wasn't the first time he'd threatened you—he'd bragged about it to me and others on the council. When Ojo left you and moved in with. . . ." Mora stopped, then looked at Ben and Henry who waited for him to finish. ". . . another woman," he continued. "Only four hundred of us live in the pueblo. Not much happens we don't know about."

He paused and glanced at Kate, hands folded in her lap. Her strong face was uplifted, a proudness filled her eyes. Then he continued. "We've handled this ourselves—the local sheriff hasn't been informed about the incident. We don't like to involve outsiders unless it goes beyond the borders of the pueblo. As you know, we have the legal right to rule on this."

A man stood, filled a cup with coffee and offered it to Kate who shifted in her chair.

"Gilbert went to see Ojo this morning," Mora resumed. "They had a long talk. Ojo knows what will happen if he ever sets foot on your place again. Gilbert took Ojo's pistol just in case."

Kate exhaled slowly, relieved that something had been done.

"I've asked an elder to purify your house next week with smudge sticks. After what Ojo did, we feel it should be done." Mora mashed out the cigarette, coughed, then called out Henry's name in a low, firm voice.

Yes?" said Henry with surprise.

"I've spoken with the council, and also with Kate. We've thought about it long and hard. You're a worry to your mother—she says you're almost never home and your grades last year were at the bottom of the class."

Henry swallowed and looked around the room at the men, who he felt were staring through his skull.

"Henry, we here in the pueblo stand together. We've been here for a thousand years. We're a proud people. We care deeply for our brothers and sisters. If someone's got a problem, we try and help. What we've decided is for your own good."

Henry didn't move. He feared what Mora was about to say. He closed his eyes, then his lips tightened into thin, straight lines. His jaw clenched as Mora stood and walked toward him. Henry's fingers gripped the chair. A thought raced through his mind—to leave in the night like Ojo, but he knew they would track him down. He felt like a trapped animal locked inside a cage. Rage filled his heart as Mora moved closer.

40

"You're going to the Indian school in Santa Fe. You've been enrolled. There's nothing to discuss," said Mora.

Kate watched Henry from the corner of her eye.

"It's a prison," whispered Henry.

"No, Henry, that's not true. You take a variety of classes and there's arts, crafts, all kinds of things. Make friends with kids from other pueblos, other nations. They come from all over, even Canada," added Mora.

"How long do I stay?" asked Henry as he struggled with his fury.

"At least a year. Depends on how you do. Kate will come to visit," said Mora who glanced at Kate as she leaned closer to Henry.

"You'll like it Henry," she said quietly then added, "I'll come to see you."

Henry tugged at the buttons on his shirt. Then Mora glanced at Ben.

"Ben?"

"Yes?"

"You're going too. Kate thinks you need a change, to see more of the world. Learn things they can't teach you here."

Pain shot through Ben like a bullet as he straightened in the chair. Stunned, he couldn't believe what he had heard. It must be a dream, he thought, like Ojo in the kitchen with the broken bottle. Had Kate stopped loving him? What had he done? He knew his grades were good, better than most. He felt betrayed, and looked away when Kate turned to speak.

"Ben? Ben?" she repeated.

He stared beyond Mora, to the tribal flag standing at attention in the corner. The fan continued to purr, shuffling smoke across the room and out the window. He couldn't speak. His heart was broken into pieces, like Ojo's bottle on the kitchen floor. Moisture formed in his eyes. Then he felt Kate's fingers touch his shoulder.

"It will be a nice change, Ben. The school will be good for you. You'll be home for the dances on San Diego's feast day, November twelfth, then Christmas is just around the corner."

The fan whirled. Ben stared at the floor beneath his shoes. Henry glared at Mora, then Kate stood and waited for the boys who left the smoke filled room in single file, followed by Kate who prayed, as they made their way through the hills toward their home beside the river.

THREE

L eon felt the cool autumn air seep through the window of the pickup. The engine throbbed as they struggled up the hill, past the opera and the elegant homes on Circle Drive perched above the valley. Kate was seated in the front. In the back, Ben and Henry leaned against the tailgate.

At the crest where Circle Drive joined the highway, Leon braked for the sharp descent through the hills which circled Santa Fe. He turned on Cerrillos Road, then slowed for the sign which read, "Deaf School," the crossing marked with signs which warned of students who were hearing impaired.

Several blocks further, Ben saw the buildings through the trees and the sweep of emerald lawns which seemed to stretch forever. Then he saw the sign above the entrance, "Santa Fe Indian School." Leon parked in the driveway. Kate stood quietly by the truck and waited for the boys, who were reluctant to say goodbye. Henry eyed the imposing building which faced the drive.

Ben finally spoke, "You're coming back, mother?"

"Yes. They said to wait awhile before I come. I'll miss you both," said Kate as she leaned and kissed the boys.

Ben and Henry watched the truck disappear in the traffic, then clutched their bags and made their way down the long dark hallway with its polished floor and high wooden doors.

"You must be the Touchstones?" said a deep voice which echoed off the plaster walls. They stopped. He was tall, heavyset, with papers in his hands. He waited quietly at the end of the corridor, then spoke again, "I'm Raymond Torres, superintendent of the school. Leave your things with me, then join the others in the gymnasium."

Ben and Henry followed his directions to the cavern of a room which smelled of sweat. They settled in hard metal chairs. Then an old man dressed in dark slacks and white embroidered shirt limped slowly to the microphone. His gray, clouded eyes scanned the room, filled with faces of many generations which had followed him. As he leaned against his cane, a hush descended on the room. He coughed, then raised his trembling hand.

"I'm Oku Pin. To you who don't speak Tewa, it means Turtle Mountain. I was born at San Juan Pueblo, before most of your parents came to be." He coughed and wiped his mouth, then shifted his weight on the cane. "As I look around, I see the future of our people staring back at me. You are one people. We are one people. I don't have many days left, but as I look at you, my heart leaps like a deer with joy and hope, that you will pull together and be family."

All eyes were riveted on the elder from San Juan, bent and frail, his face creased like saddle leather.

"You were given candles when you entered. When I call your name, then your tribe's name, light them."

Suddenly the gymnasium was plunged into darkness. The students gasped, then Oku Pin began to call their names in a strong, clear voice; "Tapia. . . Pojoaque Pueblo, Dasheno. . . Santa Clara, Humatewa. . . Hopi, Vigil. . . Nambe, Martinez. . . San Ildefonso, Hustito. . . Zuni, Touchstone. . . Tesuque." As he called the names, the room grew brighter. He continued: "Harjo. . . Lakota Sioux, Histia. . . Acoma, Yazzie. . . Navajo, Lucero. . . Isleta, Bull Tail. . . Kiowa, Yates. . . Nambe, Goldtooth. . . Choctaw, Raining Good. . . Osage."

Ben and Henry glanced around the room at the soft circles of light which grew and framed the faces surrounding them.

Oku Pin steadied himself and resumed: "Garcia . . . San Juan, Nightingale . . . Cherokee, Mermejo . . . Picuris, Red Stone . . . Chichasaw, Luhan . . . Taos." The old man droned through the list. A few had come as far away as Canada. Soon, five hundred flames merged and danced before their eyes, staring at each other through the silence.

"Now you see what we can do," said Oku Pin in a proud, firm manner. "Come together as family. Stand together and light the way for each of us. Education is the key. We ask the Great Spirit, the Spirit of our forefathers to guide us through the darkness."

A moment later, floodlights illuminated the room. A short, thin woman approached the microphone. Oku Pin stepped aside. She pushed back her auburn hair then cleared her throat. "I'm Barbara Duran. Welcome to the Indian School of Santa Fe. I'm in charge of housing, counseling and discipline. The boys will live on the first floor of each dormitory, the girls will have the top. Your meals are served three times a day in the cafeteria. You'll be responsible for your laundry, cleaning your rooms and personal hygiene. Assignments for upkeep of the property will be given to you later this afternoon. Failure to comply with any of our rules will mean a reprimand. After three of these, you'll be on probation. One more, then you're suspended and sent home. If your parents wish, they may return you to the school, but only after meeting with Mr. Torres and myself. Please stand."

Ben looked at Henry who cursed then whispered, "I knew it. I said it was a prison."

By three o'clock, Ben had met his roommate from Taos Pueblo. Dark, short and slightly built, he'd introduced himself as Luhan One. He referred to his cousin down the hall as Luhan Two. Ben noticed the long scar above his eyebrow but decided not to mention it—if Luhan One wanted to discuss it, then he would listen.

By four, Henry had settled in his room which overlooked the driveway. At six he left for dinner. He waited with his tray, steam rising from the serving line, more food than most of them had ever seen. Minutes later Ben arrived. He took his place in line, then found Henry alone, eating in the corner.

"Henry, where's your room?" Ben asked as he approached. A half-filled bottle of catsup and a vase of yellow, plastic flowers formed the centerpiece.

"Montoya Hall. Where's yours?"

"Middle Hall. Who's your roommate?"

"Don't know his name. Doesn't say much," Henry said dryly as he tasted the hot potato soup with his finger. "He's a Sioux from somewhere up north," he added slowly while licking his finger. "And he's dark, dark like a real Indian," he declared with sarcasm before he leaned to smell the broccoli. "Had to make my bed. Didn't know how. Mother always. . . ."

"I know Henry, I know. Had to make mine too. The food's pretty good."

"It's O.K. I want some fry bread and posole. This is white man's food, it's gummy."

"There's plenty of it."

"I guess."

They ate in silence and watched the others move through the line then settle in groups around the room. Ben turned and studied the brightly painted murals on the walls depicting tribal dances. The noise built as he glanced around the room, filled with students from almost every tribe in North America.

"Do you know about the showers?" asked Henry.

"What about them?"

"You have to wash in front of everybody. Naked."

"So what?" replied Ben as he smeared catsup on the meat loaf.

"Never done that. At home. . . ."

"We're not at home Henry. Mother wants us here, there's a reason for it. Don't ask me what it is, but stop complaining."

Henry wiped his mouth, stood, then shot a glare across the crowded room.

"Bullshit, this is bullshit," he snapped, then left and made his way across the lawn toward the dormitory.

Purple clouds stretched across the mountains which circled Santa Fe. Traffic on Cerrillos Road had settled to a murmur as Henry paused to watch the sunset. The hallway was empty. He stopped and heard music coming from his room. Standing in the doorway, he saw the dark skinned boy sitting on the bed in his underwear, an empty glass propped beside his leg. Henry watched smoke curl from the thin roll of paper packed with black tobacco which hung from the young boy's lips.

"Come in Henry. Close the door. I've been waiting," said the boy who sucked at the tobacco. Henry winced, but moved closer to the bed. He motioned for Henry to draw the shade.

"They said no smoking in the dormitory."

"Screw 'em," said the boy who flicked ashes on the sheet, then fixed his eyes on Henry. "My friends back home call me Ota K'te."

Henry stared at the feather shoved into his coal black hair and the onyx eyes which shot through Henry like arrows. "What's that mean?" asked Henry in a hushed voice.

"In Lakota it means Plenty Kill. When I was seven, I killed a wolf that ate our sheep. Killed it with my bare hands, then skinned it with my knife. That night my father named me."

Henry's eyes grew wide, then Plenty Kill handed him the cigarette. Henry cradled it between his fingers then brought it to his lips.

"Suck in hard, then hold it in your lungs," said Plenty Kill who reached beneath the blanket.

"It's strong. Never smoked before. But some of my friends at the pueblo do."

"Who are your people?" asked Plenty Kill as he filled the glass.

"Tesuque, just north of here."

"Born there?"

45

"Yeah. Grew up there. I'm a full blood. . . can't you tell?"

"Yeah, I thought so. Who was that white boy you were eating with awhile ago? Looks like he works here."

"Never met him. He just sat down."

Plenty Kill nodded then offered the glass to Ben.

"What's that?"

"Mescal. From Mexico. They make it out of cactus. Good stuff. See the worm?" Henry raised the glass and stared at the small white creature, curled into a ball, resting on the bottom.

"It means it's good stuff. Plenty strong. If the worm's not pickled, it's no good to drink. Try it."

Henry felt dizzy from the cigarette. He moved the glass closer to his mouth then closed his eyes. The mescal burned his throat, then travelled to his stomach. He sipped again while staring at the worm, which seemed to move.

"Now eat it Henry. It proves you're a man," said Plenty Kill who smiled as Henry continued to watch the insect drift closer to his mouth. Suddenly, he tilted back his head and felt the worm on his tongue, then it scraped against his throat. He clinched his teeth then gasped for breath.

"Good, Henry. Have another glass," said Plenty Kill who lit another cigarette and handed it to Henry on the floor, his legs crossed, just like Plenty Kill, who was staring at the wall.

Henry dropped the pencil and looked around the room. Most of them were dark as he was, others were the color of milk stained with coffee. Only two were white; a girl seated near the back and a boy across from Henry who picked at a blister on his lip.

Whoever was behind him smelled like urine. The girl in front, her pony tail secured by rubber bands, wrote something on the desktop.

"Henry Touchstone?" inquired the dark haired woman behind glasses, which to Henry seemed like cola bottles.

Henry nodded.

"See me after class, we need to talk."

"Can't. Got to clean my room, then rake leaves," snapped Henry.

"Never mind the leaves. Don't go until we've spoken. Class dismissed." Henry didn't move when she approached but continued to look straight ahead as if she wasn't there. Then she dropped the transcript on the desk beside his elbow.

"Look at it Henry. It's your grades they sent from your school in Santa Clara. They're not good."

"Good enough."

"Henry, you've got to understand. Barely passing will get you nowhere. To get ahead, you need to study and raise your grades. Then you can go to college."

"And do what?"

"Find a good job. There's plenty of things for you to do if you put your mind to it."

"That's the Anglo way. I want to make it on my own, like my ancestors. They never needed a degree from college."

"That was true a hundred years ago Henry, but now the world is different. It will pass you by. Look at Mr. Torres. He was born poor, in the Acoma Pueblo. Came to school here, then went to the university in Albuquerque. Got a degree in education and now he runs this place. He has a wife, kids, and owns a home."

Henry didn't hear a word, but thought of Plenty Kill, and how good it felt when the mescal landed in his stomach.

Weeks passed and the tribes found a rhythm of their own. The northern tribes stuck together; the tribes from the west decided they were smarter and closed ranks. The Zuni kept their distance from the Navajo, and the Hopis found themselves included by the pueblos who mingled with them all. And there were children from interracial marriages, "blacks" some called them, with different features and soft, curly hair. Ben observed they had it worse than any of the others. He felt badly for them. No one took them in. They were outcasts in the sand, existing on an island of rejection shared by all of them.

From his window Ben studied the flower gardens, flecks of color in a lawn which had turned the color of adobe. He recalled what the elder from San Juan had told them: "Come together as a family. Stand together and light the way for each of us." At that moment, Ben decided they were all one in spirit, no matter what their color. They were his brothers and sisters. They'd become his family.

A moment later, Ben noticed someone working in the garden near the dormitory. He watched for several minutes, then thought of the garden behind his house, abandoned and probably filled with weeds. The man was tall and to Ben, his arms and shoulders seemed like boulders. But there was something in the way the man worked the earth which reminded Ben of how he tilled his garden in Tesuque. Slow, quiet motions, nothing hurried. To Ben there seemed a gentleness in the way he labored with the soil, as if he cared. The man suddenly straightened, then turned as he sensed someone was watching. Ben continued to stare. The man smiled and wiped his face lathered with sweat. A zinnia, white as snow, dropped from his hand. He bent and pulled another until the flowers lay in heaps beneath his boots. Ben watched them disappear from the beds. Nothing remained except the dark earth which the man began to spade. His hands were rough. His face was the color of the sand which he churned into the soil. He turned again and smiled at Ben, then pointed to a pitchfork propped against the wheelbarrow.

Ben left the window, hurried down the hall and out the door.

"Want to help, boy?" said the man without turning.

"Yes. I've got a garden at my house. It's a vegetable garden. I grow chilies and sell them at the market," said Ben between breaths. The man straightened. Ben waited. Then he pointed to the pitchfork and said, "If you want to help me till this dirt, I'd be grateful."

Ben began to work. He guessed the man to be forty, maybe fifty, he really couldn't tell. His eyes were brown and wrinkled at the edges. The undershirt was stained from sweat which trickled down the handle of his shovel.

"What's your name, boy?"

"Ben, Ben Touchstone. What's yours?"

"Nando."

"Nando? That's all?"

"Short for Fernando. That's enough."

"You work for the school?" asked Ben as he struggled with the sand.

"Have for years. Started as a boy, about your age. 'Bout the only job I can do. I keep the place up—trim hedges, cut the grass and tend the flowers. Never seem to finish."

"What are you gonna plant?" asked Ben as he rammed the pitchfork deep into the soil.

48

"Pansies. 'Bout the only thing with color that can live through the winter. Ben, you work the soil like you know what you're doing. Nice and easy like."

"My father Ojo taught me."

"Ojo? Ojo, the eye. Now that's a name! Are you a mixed breed?"

"Yes, my father's Tesuque, my mother's Anglo."

"Are they both alive?"

"Mother lives alone. Ojo left us."

"I'm sorry Ben. That happens. But things work out, they always do," said Nando as he rolled the wheelbarrow, heavy with sand, closer to the beds. For several hours they mixed sand into the soil while sharing endless stories. Ben felt good working with his hands, his feet buried in the earth.

"It's three o'clock, Nando. I've got to go to class then clean my room."

"Can you come again?" asked Nando while he rested on the handle of the shovel.

"I'd like that."

"Meet me tomorrow afternoon. We'll work the other beds, then start to plant the pansies."

That evening, Ben lay in bed and thought about the afternoon spent with Nando. He'd met someone older he could talk with. They both liked working with the earth and Ben sensed a kindness in his voice, like Ojo's before he started drinking. He closed his eyes and prayed that his angel was watching over Kate, alone in the house beside the river.

The following day, his classes seemed eternal. Ben thought of Nando and the work which lay ahead. He'd never even seen a pansy, but knew that Nando would be patient.

"Viola Wittrockiana," Nando said proudly, later in the day as cool wind stirred the bare limbs above their heads. He rolled up the collar of his jacket then handed Ben the pansy, its petals the color of an apricot.

"Viola what?"

"Wittrockiana," Nando repeated then stooped to carve a hole in the soft black soil. "Viola is the genus, Ben. Wittrockiana is the species."

Ben held the small plant closer to his face and touched the petals which felt like velvet.

"How do you know the name?" asked Ben as he continued to examine the delicate looking flower.

"Started reading about them when I was about your age. Flowers and plants, that's all I read about now. No newspapers, don't even own a television. Over the years I've come to learn a lot about them."

Ben knelt and positioned the flower in the ground.

"Cover up the roots, then pack the dirt tight around the stems." Nando watched Ben's fingers press against the soil. "Well done," he said, then handed him another pansy, deep blue, which almost matched Ben's eyes.

"Now bring some flats and start your rows. Set them a foot apart. When they grow, they spread and fill the bare spots," said Nando who knelt across from Ben, who had already planted four.

Several minutes later Ben asked in a quiet voice, "Nando, do you ever go to church?" Ben reached into the flat beside his knee while he waited for Nando's reply.

"Almost every day. There's Mass in the chapel, didn't you know?"

"Here? Here at school?"

"Yes, at eight. An old priest from the cathedral comes every morning."

"I'm a Catholic too. My mother takes us every Sunday to the church at the pueblo. Then on Christmas Eve we walk up to Chimayo."

"Where the sacred dirt is?" asked Nando, his heavy fingers running quickly through the soil.

"Yeah. You know about it?"

"Everyone up here knows about Chimayo. When I was real young I had a limp, a bad one. All kinds of doctors looked me over. Said there was nothing they could do. Then my parents took me to Chimayo and rubbed the sacred dirt across my leg. That night I ran into the kitchen. They all just stared, then they cried. They cried all night. The next day we returned and mother hung my crutches on the wall beside the statue of the Santo Niño."

After a long pause Ben glanced at Nando. "Do you believe in angels?" he asked, in a voice so small that Nando barely heard him.

"Angels?"

"Yes, angels," repeated Ben just above a whisper.

"Well. . . I've never seen one, but they say that they exist."

"Can you keep a secret?"

Nando nodded.

"I've seen mine, Nando. One night on Christmas Eve, at Chimayo. In the same room where you were healed. She was young and beautiful. Her eyes were the color of the sea. And she sounded gentle, gentle as a doe."

Nando straightened then stared at Ben who knelt to dig another hole. He watched him for several minutes, then stood.

"I believe you Ben."

Ben stopped and looked up at Nando, a tower of a figure, his massive hands covered with thick, black dirt.

Ben was startled. "You do?" he said.

"Why not?"

"Then you're the only one who believes me. My brother Henry laughed. My mother wouldn't even talk about it. The old priest at Chimayo thinks I'm dreaming." Ben turned away and lowered his eyes to the pansies which spanned the garden.

"Ben, I want you to listen to me. Keep believing in your angel. Nowadays people are believing in the wrong things."

"Like what?" asked Ben.

"Like money, power, selfishness. Now people kill each other over anything, even for a thrill."

"That's what my friend Luther says—people don't respect each other anymore, let alone the animals, forests and the rivers."

"Your friend's right, Ben. The world's gone mad. You'll do just fine by sticking with your angel. Now it's time you wash and get to dinner."

Ben stood, then walked slowly up the drive. He thought about what Nando had said and turned to wave, but Nando wasn't there.

He felt warm inside. For the first time in his life, someone had listened to the thoughts within his heart.

For the next two days between classes, Ben took the sidewalk which would lead him closer to the flower beds. Nando had told him he'd never missed a day of work in twenty years. On the third day, he left the sidewalk and crossed the lawn toward the cafeteria, then made his way up the highest hill on campus. It was then he saw the greenhouse almost hidden in the cottonwoods, their amber leaves whipped by the first cold gusts of autumn.

He quietly approached the door and watched Nando sorting boxes. Nando placed row after row on the counter, then wrote something in a book. Without turning, Nando said, "Come in Ben. I was hoping you'd find the greenhouse. I've been busy sorting bulbs."

"Bulbs?" repeated Ben. "What's bulbs?"

"Come closer, I'll show you." Nando opened up the first two boxes then pointed to the tulip bulbs, brown and withered.

"They're onions. We used to plant them in my garden."

"No, Ben, they're tulip bulbs. I plant them now, and in the spring they break ground and start to bloom."

"Really?" said Ben softly.

"Yes, really. See the different shapes and sizes?"

"Yeah."

"Most of these are tulips. Some are daffodils. Even got some crocus." Nando reached for a bulb and held it between his thick, wide fingers. "These are called Flaming Parrot. They got big ruffled blooms. These ones here are called Rembrandt. Lots of colors. They call those over there Gudoshniks. Strange name. Their blooms are red and orange."

Ben touched the bulbs and tried to imagine such colors coming from something so ugly and misshapen. Nando stooped to open another box beneath the counter. "But these are my favorite. Come see." Ben leaned and stared into the mound of bulbs which still appeared to him like onions. "What are these things?"

"Darwin tulips," Nando said proudly.

"Never heard of them."

"Long stems, with the brightest red blooms you ever saw. Redder than a tomato. In this climate they only bloom once, then they die. Here, keep one." Ben held the egg-shaped root closer to his face, smelled it, then dropped it in his pocket. Nando reached into a box, then scribbled in the notebook. As he wrote, he said, "Ben, I've never figured out how people can grow flowers and not believe in God."

"Never thought of it before," replied Ben who wiped his face from the sticky warmth which filled the greenhouse. "But I think I see what you mean. These things are ugly now, but in the spring, they must be beautiful."

"They are Ben, they are."

"That's almost like a miracle. Maybe that's how God made us. Some of us are ugly, and some of us aren't. I bet God wants all of us to bloom."

"Exactly, to show the beauty inside all of us," added Nando as he leaned to trim a rosebush.

Ben thought while he watched Nando work. "Nando, why are people mean to each other?"

"Who's mean?"

"The people that. . . ." Ben paused.

"What people, Ben?" Nando asked as he added soil to a pot bursting with geraniums.

"Some people look at me funny, then turn away. The worst is when they ignore me, as if I wasn't there. They can't figure me out. They think all Indians should be the color of adobe." Ben stared at the geraniums, but Nando saw the sadness in his eyes.

"Don't mind those people, Ben. They aren't happy. They look down on others who are different, to make themselves feel better. They're the loneliest people in the world. I should know Ben. I'm Hispanic, my skin is a whole lot darker than adobe."

Ben cut his cobalt eyes to Nando then blinked. "They're mean in other ways too."

"How, Ben?"

"Ojo, my father, treats my mother terrible. He left us in the middle of the night. And Henry, my brother. He never says anything nice to me or anybody else. I think he hates everyone. Why do people act like that?"

"They're missing something inside, Ben."

"A heart?"

"No, Ben, love. Love is hard to talk about, but if you have it inside, you know it's there. You have it Ben, I can tell."

"You think so?"

"I'm sure of it. But don't ever lose it, Ben. If you lose love, you've lost everything."

"Everything?" asked Ben in a whisper.

"Yes, everything." Nando straightened, then turned to Ben, who touched the tulip bulb through the lining of his pocket. "Ben, I want to tell you something." Ben stared into Nando's faded eyes, filled with gentleness. "I have a feeling about you, Ben. I sense great things will happen in your life. Good people will surround you, but others will show you things so bad, you'd never dreamed such things existed. Stay strong, Ben. Listen to your heart and remember what I've told you."

Ben turned away, disturbed by what Nando had said.

"It's time I get home. If you want, meet me in the garden tomorrow after class, the one by the entrance. I'd be obliged if you'd help, there's hundreds of bulbs to plant."

Nando watched Ben move slowly through the cottonwoods. Ben leaned and said a prayer for Nando, reached into his pocket, then gently shoved the bulb beneath the soil.

A month passed. It was the first week in November and Ben grimaced from the frigid wind which swept down from the mountains. As he quickly made his way across the campus, he clutched the note which read: "Report to Miss Duran at ten o'clock." He shoved his hands into his jeans and glanced at the thick, gray sky while he hurried to her office.

"Sit down Ben."

Henry sat quietly across the room, his hands folded in his lap.

"First, I want you to know that your mother is fine. There's no need for you to worry," said Barbara Duran from behind the glass-topped desk.

Both boys shot a glance at each other then fixed their eyes on Duran.

"I just got a call from Gilbert Zuniga, the tribal police chief in Tesuque." Ben's breath quickened. Henry looked away toward the corner.

"Your father Ojo came to your house last night. He was very drunk. He woke your mother. She wouldn't let him in, so he blew the door down with his shotgun. It's not clear what happened next, but your father ran when he saw a man standing in your driveway. Your mother's fine. A woman named Ocate is staying with her. She said to tell you not to worry. She's calling you tonight."

Ben's fingers gripped the chair before he spoke, "Where's Ojo?"

"The police went directly to his house at the pueblo. He wasn't there. They've formed a search party. He's nowhere to be found. They think he's on the run."

Ben asked anxiously, "Did you talk to mother?"

"For just a minute. She sounded fine, just tired. She said for you not to worry."

"That bastard," whispered Ben.

"But since you're both here, we need to discuss something."

Henry looked at Ben. Ben stared at Duran who tapped a pencil on the desk.

"Ben, your grades are improving. You could do better if you tried harder. You're mixing with the others and I see you've signed up for a painting class."

Ben nodded as she turned to Henry.

"Henry. Henry look at me!" she snapped.

Henry's dark eyes flashed. His lips tightened, then the muscles in his jaw began to flex.

"Henry, you're grades are bad and getting worse. The teachers tell me you're late for class. You haven't made friends. The only boy you hang around with is your roommate who calls himself Plenty Kill." Henry shifted in his chair as she continued. "A teacher says she smelled liquor on your breath. Another saw you smoking after class behind the gym."

Ben stared at Henry in disbelief. "You've been smoking and drinking? Is that true?" he asked angrily.

"Since when do you care? Don't mess with me. Leave me alone."

Ben straightened in the chair. "I've had it. I hope mother never knows what you've been doing. If she finds out, it would kill her. Try and think about her for a change," shouted Ben.

Duran interrupted, "Ben, let me speak. Henry, I'm putting you on probation. Tomorrow afternoon you're moving to another dormitory. In the morning you'll meet with one of our counsellors. You'll see him every day for an hour. You've got an attitude problem Henry, a bad one, and if it doesn't change, I'm calling your mother to come and take you home. Have I made myself clear?"

Henry didn't answer, but glared at the floor, his fingers tightened into fists.

"Is that clear?" she repeated in a loud voice. Henry slowly turned his head then stared across the room at Ben. Hate surged through his heart then filled his face as he stood and left the room in silence.

In his room that night, Henry reached for the bottle rolled in a sweater at the bottom of the dresser. Plenty Kill was propped against the pillow, a cigarette dangled from his lip.

Henry filled the glass and slumped in the corner, his head against the wall.

"I've been thinking Henry."

"About what?"

"I figured a way for us to get some extra money. You know the office in the cafeteria? They keep money in there."

"Yeah?" said Henry as he passed the glass of mescal to Plenty Kill.

"There's a window. I've checked it out. Nobody will see us. It backs up to the trees."

"You gonna break in?"

"No, Henry, we are. Tonight. Are you with me?"

"Got nothin' to lose. Duran put me on probation. I'm moving out tomorrow. The bitch says she's sending me to a counsellor. This place sucks."

"Keep your voice down, Henry. We get caught drinking and they'll throw us both out. Give me the bottle." After several sips, Plenty Kill held a finger to his mouth, then motioned for Henry to move closer. He lowered his voice and stared at Henry, his dark eyes boring holes through Henry's forehead.

"Before we go, there's something I got to know. Best friends don't lie to each other, do they Henry?"

"I've never lied to you Plenty Kill."

"Your brother's a half breed. That makes you a half breed. The first night I saw you with him in the cafeteria, you said you didn't know him. You're a scum sucking half breed just like Ben."

Henry's eyes dropped to the floor. Plenty Kill lit another cigarette.

"Henry, I'm gonna let you make it up for lying to me. Let's find out if you're my friend and if you're a man, a real man. I need to know."

Henry watched Plenty Kill slowly draw the knife from under the pillow. The blade was long, its edge shimmered like a razor. He stood and moved closer to Henry who backed into the corner.

"Ever hear of cutting?"

"No," said Henry as he pressed himself against the wall.

"It's something I thought up. Cut yourself Henry. Proves you're a man afraid of 'nothin. Got the stomach for it?"

Plenty Kill placed the knife in Henry's hand. Smoke curled from his flared nostrils as he watched Henry move the blade closer to his wrist. Sweat crossed Henry's mouth. Suddenly, Henry closed his eyes and slashed, then slashed again. Blood spurted on the floor. Henry screamed. Plenty Kill placed his hand on Henry's mouth, then grabbed the sheet.

"Shit! You cut too deep Henry. Wrap it with the sheet. You'll bleed to death."

Henry felt the warm blood ooze between his fingers as Plenty Kill quickly tied the torn sheet around his wrist.

"Let's get moving. Bed check's in half an hour. Move it Henry."

At nine that evening Kate called.

"So everything's O.K.? Are you sure? Is Mrs. Ocate still there? I'll get Henry. Wait ten minutes then call us back. I love you."

Ben ran from the dormitory and out into the cold night air, crossed the lawn and raced toward Montoya Hall. He moved quickly down the darkened corridor, lit by a ruby colored lamp which glowed above the fire door. At the end of the hall, he stopped. The names, "Touchstone" and "Harjo" were printed on a card beside the door.

He knocked. He knocked again. Ben pressed his ear against the door and heard someone talking on the radio.

"Henry, it's Ben. Open the door. I spoke with mother, she wants to talk to you. Open up." He slowly turned the handle then froze. A pool of blood was at his feet. A crimson circle filled the center of the bed. He rushed down the hall and saw more blood leading to the fire door. The terrifying images came quickly—of Henry dying somewhere, bleeding from a stab wound. Ben raced down the sidewalk. Lights in the trees flooded the courtyard. The small red dots led him further down the hill toward the cafeteria. Ben's chest heaved, his heart was in his throat. Then he saw two figures crouched in the shadow of the building.

He moved closer. Henry stood and faced him.

"Henry, is that you? Is that you Henry?"

"Stay away Ben. This is none of your business!" shrieked Henry.

"The blood?" Ben stopped and stared at the cloth tied around Henry's wrist, then saw his face—twisted, seething with hatred. Henry's eyes glowed hot, like cinders. Ben hardly recognized his brother.

"Back off Ben. I've got nothin' to lose. Plenty Kill's got a knife. I'm warning you."

At that instant, Ben saw something move through the shadows and rush toward them. Suddenly, Plenty Kill raised the knife above his head. The figure lunged at Plenty Kill and hurled him to the ground. The boy screamed and struggled to his feet. The figure wheeled as his massive fist struck Plenty Kill between the eyes. The knife tumbled from his hand. Henry froze and stared at Plenty Kill, unconscious, sprawled across the sidewalk.

Then Ben saw the face—dark brown wrinkled eyes and skin the color of sand. "Nando! What the—"

"I was leaving the greenhouse when I heard voices. Then I saw the boy raise the knife." Nando turned and saw Henry standing over Plenty Kill, the bloody cloth wrapped around his wrist. "He'll come around. You're hurt, you need to see a doctor."

The cold wind shook the branches. A low cloud raced behind the moon. A sadness swept through Ben as he watched Henry disappear into the shadows. He realized that his days at the Indian school had ended. Ben knew he'd miss Nando and the afternoon discussions in the gardens.

Nando heard Ben say quietly, "He's my brother. I'll call mother in the morning. I've got to take him home."

FOUR

Amelia Ocate left the engine running while Kate signed the papers. Henry sat in the back seat, his sleeve rolled above the wound the nurse had dressed the night before. Amelia glanced in the mirror at Henry who was staring at the bandage.

"What happened Henry?" she asked.

"Nothin'. Just an accident."

Henry watched Ben and Kate move slowly down the steps toward the gray Chevrolet, their breaths forming clouds in the cold morning air. Kate pulled the collar of the coat closer to her neck. Her head was bent. Ben hooked his arm through Kate's elbow as they neared the car. Henry touched the bandage, then saw Amelia staring in the mirror.

Ben closed the door for Kate and joined Henry in the back. At the entrance, he saw Nando by the hedge with clippers moving slowly in his hands. Ben waved. Nando never saw him.

The car accelerated and blended with the traffic on Cerrillos Road. They passed the cemetery, long rows of small white crosses which marked the graves of soldiers. Next, the homes nestled in the hills, spotted with piñon trees and cedars, then the grand houses on Circle Drive which overlooked the valley.

Kate called Henry's name as they passed the outdoor opera, jutting from the rocks above the highway.

"Henry, answer mother," said Ben.

"What?" snapped Henry as the car droned toward Tesuque.

"Miss Duran told me everything. About your drinking and the smoking. And the 'cutting ceremony,' she called it. It's going to stop Henry, do you understand?"

"Yes ma'am."

"Mrs. Sanchez at your school in Santa Clara, said she'll take you back. You'll both lose half a year, but there's nothing else to do."

"Have you heard where Ojo is?" asked Ben.

"They haven't found him. He's run away. Just as good. I never want to see his face again," said Kate firmly.

Amelia Ocate slowed at the sign which read, "Billco Carpets," then turned onto the narrow road which would lead them home.

Ben helped Kate up the stairs to the porch, then asked, "Who fixed the door?"

"Gilbert Zuniga. He hung a new one the morning after Ojo. . . " said Kate, her words trailing off as Ben slumped into the kitchen chair. Henry dropped his bag and disappeared into the bathroom. Amelia Ocate hugged Kate, talked for several minutes then said goodbye.

The house was quiet. Only the sound of cold, November wind howling across the roof.

"I was told someone frightened Ojo," said Ben from the kitchen table. "Who was it mother?"

"Don't know. Ojo was outside on the porch screaming. He wanted to take you and Henry. It was horrible. He said he'd blow the door down and take you both at gunpoint if I didn't let him in. Then someone called his name. I looked out the window and saw a man in the driveway with a pistol. Ojo fired the shotgun at the door, then leveled it on the man who shouted something. Then Ojo disappeared."

Ben looked away before he said, "I guess the garden's frozen over?" He stood and crossed the kitchen.

"I'm sure it is," sighed Kate as she filled a pot with beans and water. "I cleaned it up. Raked the weeds. I knew you'd be home for the dances next week." After a long pause she reached into the pantry and set the paper cup on the table. "I found this while I was cleaning out the garden. Thought you'd like it."

Ben shifted his attention from the window to the cup, leaned, then peered inside. His eyes grew wide when he saw the small mound of orange coral embedded in the cross. Then he saw the crow's foot stamped into the back. "It's the cross Two Crows was wearing when he pulled me from the river!" he exclaimed.

Kate stared at the cross.

"He was here!" Ben said in a rising voice. "It's got to be him! He's the man that scared Ojo away."

Kate wiped her hands and held it to the window. "It's a crow's foot all right. So the man that saved you called himself Two Crows?"

"Yes. It's the same cross. I'd know it anywhere. I'm going up to find him. To thank him."

"Up in the canyon at Cundiyo?"

"That's where he lives."

"Only if you go with someone. Ask Luther. I know he'd like to see you."

The next morning Ben joined Luther in the truck. Leon drove and said he would fish beneath the bridge while they hiked into the canyon.

An hour later the boys were standing on the trail, far above the river which had narrowed to a trickle. They climbed higher through the limestone cliffs as Ben strained to see the pool where he'd almost lost his life. He thought of Two Crows and wondered if he'd find him in the tepee near the ridge.

Luther pointed to a deer, far below beside the stream, its antlers erect. They saw the outline of a wolf stalking the ridge above the timberline and Luther recalled his dream about the wolf which killed its cubs. The heavy scent of pine and spruce filled their nostrils and Ben felt grateful for the beauty which surrounded him. He envied Two Crows; fishing, hunting, waking every morning to the splendors of the canyon.

"Ben? You coming to the feast day dances next week at the pueblo?"

"Yeah, I guess so. Are you dancing Luther?"

"For sure. This year Leon's one of the buffalo men. I'm dancing with him as an antelope. Gonna wear Leon's antelope horns that his father gave him when he was just a boy."

"You think Ojo will come?" asked Ben as he struggled up the incline.

"No way. He won't show. He knows better. Too many people were looking for him. How much further?" asked Luther who reached into his pack for fry bread which he broke and shared with Ben. "You hiked a hell of a long way that morning after the storm. We've been on this trail forever," said Luther as he chewed the soft, moist bread.

The boys increased their pace as they approached the timberline, a thousand feet above the trail. "Two Crows' tepee is up there, beyond that stand of aspens, where the trees won't grow," said Ben as he pointed. Their breaths became harder to draw and from the scarcity of flora, Ben knew they'd passed ten thousand feet, maybe higher. "Another quarter mile, Luther, I promise."

They trudged toward the ridge, then stopped to rest.

The trail ended at the clearing. A meadow lay before them filled with dry, brown stems, bent toward the ground. "It's almost winter. Didn't expect to find the flowers," said Ben through his heavy breath, "they were beautiful when I was here before."

Several minutes later, Ben suddenly stopped. "Something's wrong, Luther. I'd swear the tepee was here. I remember it clearly. That morning, I stood outside the entrance and saw this meadow. And those aspens down there, they were here too."

Luther followed Ben as he walked through the tall weeds toward the ridge. Ben halted. "It's gone!" he exclaimed.

"Can't be Ben. You described everything just like it was; the meadow, the aspens below us. It's all here."

"Two Crows," Ben shouted. "Two Crows! You saved my life!" His cries echoed through the gorge. He shouted once again but his words returned without an answer. Ben then stooped to clear the weeds beneath his boots. "Luther, start looking. There's bound to be something left behind. There were smooth gray rocks around the fire pit. He had a small wood table and a stove. I remember a pipe and a pouch filled with tobacco. Look for anything," said Ben anxiously.

Luther moved slowly through the tall weeds which brushed against his long, black hair. Luther searched the ground around him, then moved higher toward the ridge. Ben walked in circles near the meadow. "Ben, there's nothing here, never has been," Luther shouted from the ridge. "This ground is virgin. No one's even camped here, let alone erected a tepee. Let's forget it, it's getting late. Maybe you imagined it. Probably hit your head when you fell into the river."

Fifteen minutes passed. Ben unearthed a rusted cartridge. Luther found a deer antler which he planned to mount above his bed.

Suddenly from the ridge, Luther shouted, "Ben, Come Here!" then held the silver chain above his head. Ben rushed up the ridge and stared at the chain and broken clasp in Luther's hand. Ben reached into his jeans. "And this is the cross Two Crows wore when he pulled me from the river. Kate found it when she was cleaning out the garden. He wore it on this chain. I told you he was here."

"Are you sure?" asked Luther who glanced at his watch.

"Positive."

Luther looked down at the cross in Ben's hand, then glanced again at his watch. "We should go. Leon's waiting for us by the bridge."

Ben followed Luther through the meadow, past the aspens, then down toward the trail. While they walked, Ben sensed that Two Crows was alive, somewhere in the canyon. Maybe Luther was right, that he'd hit his head and dreamed it. But the clothes, the dinner and the bandages which Two Crows had provided? Now the cross and chain? And Luther's dreams which seemed to tell the future? He couldn't explain any of these things but would contemplate them all, for many years to come.

FIVE

L uther stood alone and proud before the sunrise, his head erect. The pueblo and the valley lay beneath him. His vision stretched for miles beyond the mountains, even further than the clouds which touched the rising sun. Later in the morning in the kiva, he would paint his face white as pearls and dance like an antelope until the sun dropped behind the water tank. But now he was alone with the Spirits of the Lake from which he came. Soon the drums would beat, and he would prance before the buffalo men. For now, though, he savored the moonset, and the stars which lingered in the dawn above Tesuque.

It was the feast of San Diego. The pueblo woke to sounds of children playing in the narrow dirt streets which crisscrossed, then backtracked to the plaza and the church. Smoke rose from piñon fires which warmed the low adobe dwellings.

Ben struggled from bed in his house across the river, dressed and soon was standing in the plaza, waiting for Mass to begin. San Diego would be happy, he thought, as his eyes darted around the crowds which began to build. Cars streamed toward the pueblo from the Taos highway. Some came from other pueblos, others from Santa Fe, and some, rented by tourists, arrived from the Albuquerque airport. All were welcomed by the people of Tesuque.

The morning air was thick with pungent smells; bread baking in rounded hornos, roasted chilies, biscochitos cookies and piñon fires blazing in the plaza. Kettles of green posole basked in brilliant light which poured across the valley.

From the center of the plaza Ben studied the people, which by now numbered in the hundreds. Some nibbled at tamales, fry bread and turkey, others strained to find the dancers who were hidden in the sacred kiva, away from prying eyes.

Women wearing long, bright manta skirts mingled with relatives, neighbors and friends. To Ben it seemed a thousand voices filled the plaza. Tourists spoke in languages he couldn't comprehend and he noticed some with slanted eyes who wore cameras on their belts.

Wind blew across the plaza lifting dust and papers into the air. People entered the modest homes which faced the church, then emerged with plastic plates heaped with chicken, tamales, beans and empanadas. The smell of scalded lard hovered in the air. Ben saw silver beads laced with coral and turquoise, while concha belts and bracelets glittered in the sunlight. A young boy rushed past, his face painted like a sunset on the mesa.

The bell struck once, then again. Ben covered his ears as he walked toward the small adobe church which faced the plaza. Then he saw Father Ortiz standing in the doorway, his vestments white as clouds, the worn prayer book resting in his hands.

"Ben? Haven't seen you in awhile. How do you like the Indian School in Santa Fe?"

Ben looked away before he replied, "Kate brought us home the other day."

"For the dances?"

"No, for good. Henry's got problems. They sent him home. I didn't think she could handle him alone, so I came too."

"I'm sorry to hear that Ben. The school has a fine reputation. You would have done well there."

"I suppose, but sometimes you gotta do things you don't want to."

"That's true. What did Henry do?"

"His roommate was weird. Called himself Plenty Kill. Got Henry into smoking and drinking, then told him he'd prove he was a man if he cut himself."

"Cut himself? How strange. He didn't do it, did he?"

"Sure did. Blood everywhere. I found him that night outside with Plenty Kill, who pulled his knife on me. If it weren't for Nando. . . ."

"Who's Nando?"

64

"The groundskeeper at the school. He stopped Plenty Kill just before he stabbed me. Saved my life."

"So they've suspended Henry?"

"Yeah. Mother came and got us the next morning."

"Where is Henry now?"

"At home. Mother's there now keeping an eye on him, especially today. Doesn't trust him anymore."

"I'll speak to Henry."

"Won't do any good. He's gotten worse. I think he hates the whole world."

"I'll drop by just the same. Are you coming to Mass?"

"Planned to, then I'm staying for the dances. My friend Luther's an antelope. Are you staying?"

"Of course. These are my parishioners. It's the feast day of San Diego. It's a wonderful expression of their beliefs."

"I guess. I'll see you later."

"I hope so, Ben. Tell Kate I'll be saying Mass here every Sunday morning. Father Lucido was moved to Taos."

The eighth loud clang from the bell cracked across the plaza. People began to move toward the entrance, tossing plates and cups into bins beside careworn doors which had been hung a hundred years before. They dipped their fingers into holy water, genuflected, then shuffled down the narrow aisle to take their places on the hard, wooden pews. Ben entered and chose the pew near the back of the sanctuary. The modest church would hold no more than fifty and soon it was almost filled. Glass beads hung from shriveled fingers of the old pueblo women, gray hairs were wound into chignons and their rounded shoulders were draped with dark colored sweaters. Ben's eyes moved past the matriarchs to the tiny altar and above it, the figure of Christ, thin arms and legs carved from wood blackened by decades of incense and votive candles. Ben's gaze then rested on two plaster angel figures kneeling beneath the cross, faces frozen in reverent contemplation. Without a sound, Father Ortiz entered from the sacristy, bowed before the altar then turned to face the people. The congregation stood. He cleared his throat. "On behalf of the families of Tesuque Pueblo, I welcome any visitors to our church."

The priest glanced toward the rear then motioned for everyone to sit.

"As you know this is the feast day of San Diego, patron saint of Tesuque Pueblo. In the year sixteen hundred and eight, warriors from this pueblo struck the first blow in the revolt against religious persecution. Almost eight hundred years before that, their ancestors were living by this river, three miles east from where you're sitting. They called this place, Te-Tsu-Geh, which means in Tewa, Cottonwood Tree Place because of the trees which line the river."

Ben's eyes focused on Father Ortiz, his body frail and bent, as he moved slowly from the altar toward the pews.

"Most of the families who live in the pueblo are Catholics, which may surprise some of you who are here for the first time. Look around. The person next to you probably has relatives who are now inside the sacred kiva preparing for the buffalo dance. Their faces will be painted, animal skins and horns will be strapped to their heads, kilts and sashes will be tied around their waists, then drums will beat. Just as I stand before you in these vestments of the Church, those are the vestments of a culture which has been here over a thousand years. Underneath their paint and feathers and underneath my robes, we are all the same; children of God, a God who loves us as we are. Please stand to say the Creed."

During communion the drums began to pound. Softly at first, then resounded off the ceiling and the statues whose eyes were fixed on the congregation bent in prayer. The doors creaked open and sunlight poured in. Ben dipped his finger into the holy water, then glanced at the crowds spilling into the plaza from narrow dirt streets which crisscrossed the pueblo.

The cadence of the drums intensified, like thunder in a canyon. Conversations stopped as children scurried for better views. The ground began to tremble. Out of view, the dancers moved slowly from the kiva.

Ben settled on the low adobe wall which divided the plaza from the church courtyard. He glanced down at a girl half his age, who smiled. Her eyes were as green as the malachite necklace wrapped around her neck. Her face was painted blue and yellow, a feather jutted from her slick, black hair which glistened like wet onyx. Pink clouds of cotton candy floated off her fingers.

Four men formed a circle around a large drum in the corner of the plaza, and at the center, the chorus of forty men began to chant, beginning low in their stomachs, then building to sweep through the crowd. Soon the chorus found the rhythm of the drums and it all fused into one sound. The drummers pounded steadily. The chanting blended perfectly with the drumbeats and echoed off the adobe walls which ringed the plaza. Suddenly, all eyes shifted. Ben steadied himself as he stood and balanced on the wall.

Luther entered. His face was painted white, his neck yellow. Antelope horns protruded from his head and his long black hair swayed with the drumbeats. Women appeared in long flowing manta skirts which brushed against their moccasins and their white embroidered blouses were dazzling in the sunlight.

Suddenly, four men with faces painted raven black burst into the plaza, their necks smeared white. Pale yellow kilts and sashes were wrapped around their waists. Deer antlers were fastened to their heads and as they leaned, each jabbed the ground with sticks wrapped with cedar to imitate the forelegs of the animals.

The dancers shuffled to the center of the plaza, moving with the beat of the drummers and the chorus. The hushed crowd drew close.

Ben's stare followed Luther who leaped in the air then whirled to face two dark figures staring from the corner of the plaza. The buffalo men stood erect. Their chests, arms and legs were painted black. Buffalo horns tipped with feathers jutted from their heads, covered with bison hide and hair, which continued over their shoulders, then down to the center of their backs. Black feathers sewn to the hide, stood out from their shoulders like wings. Ben admired the custard shaded kilts and crimson sashes which hung almost to their knees, and at their necks, clams shells made of turquoise. The buffalo men also moved in perfect cadence with the drums. Sun glinted off their wrists wrapped in silver bracelets. Deerskin boots, covered in bells, added a chilling sound to the drum beats. Black paint smeared their faces. The taller man's eyes flashed as he raised the bow and arrow above his head and shook the rattle. A woman, almost hidden, stood behind them, dressed in a long manta which almost touched the ground. Her neck was covered in turquoise and she waved feathers from a red-tailed hawk. She fastened her eyes on the ground, as they all moved forward to tell the story of the hunt.

The wall beneath his boots began to vibrate as Ben watched the dancing and felt transported to another world. Their feet kicked dust which whirled above the dancer's heads. Bells jangled on their legs, gourds filled with rocks rattled to the thundering drums.

The buffalo men remained upright while horned deer and antelope bent forward and sprang in all directions. The woman shuffled forward and took her place between the buffalo men and they continued to dance until the pumpkin colored sun straddled the hills west of the pueblo. The ancient legend of the plentiful hunt had been told another year, as it had been for centuries.

A chilled wind touched Ben's face. He sat alone on the low wall and watched the people leave the plaza. He wanted to join the dancers, but guessed the reason he'd never been invited. Too white, he supposed, or maybe because Ojo was his father.

Some people still milled in circles, talking with friends. Others carried plastic bags filled with tamales. Ben guessed they'd take them home for dinner. From behind, a frail voice called his name. Ben turned and saw Father Ortiz standing in the courtyard, frozen, like the statue of San Diego in the church.

"Come here Ben, I've got something for your mother," said the old man who watched Ben jump from the wall, then move through the high grass which needed cutting.

Father Ortiz leaned and stuffed the envelope into Ben's jacket, which he had quickly zipped as the wind stirred the tall, brown grass brushing against his elbows.

"A little something to help get her through the week."

Ben retrieved it and stared at the twenty dollar bill, folded neatly in the corner of the envelope.

"I keep a little back from the collection. Never know when one of my families might need it. Should buy some staples. Tell Kate I'll be by soon. I hope she's well?"

"Yeah, she's fine," said Ben as he carefully folded the bill and tucked it in his pocket. A strong gust blew across the courtyard. "Did you like the dances?" asked Father Ortiz who clutched the straw hat which fluttered above his wrinkled face. Ben stared at the weeds between his legs. Father Ortiz put his hand gently on Ben's shoulder.

"You wanted to dance, didn't you Ben?"

"Not really."

"Your best friend Luther was an antelope, wasn't he?"

"Yeah. Luther danced real good. Maybe next year," replied Ben in a distant voice. It was then Father Ortiz sensed the hurt which simmered deep within Ben.

"You'll be fifteen, then. Old enough to be an antelope, even a deer I suspect. Ask Luther."

Ben glanced up into the kind eyes of the priest who turned and walked slowly through the weeds toward the church.

Ben shifted his attention to the plaza. Only a handful of tourists remained. Soon, even they began to leave. A sand colored cat arched its back and rubbed against a doorway. The smell of hot lard lingered in his nostrils and in the corner of the plaza, an old woman jabbed papers with a stick and dropped them in a sack. On the hill which surveyed the pueblo, a coyote began to howl.

Ben stared down at his boots and tried to repress the sadness which floated somewhere between his stomach and his throat. It was too big to handle and he wanted rid of it. He felt he was in limbo, trapped between two worlds: one white, the other the color of adobe mud. No one seemed to want him, not even the friends he'd known since he could walk. He felt the old priest understood, and Kate. She always understood, even when he didn't.

Ben sat on the wall until it was too dark to see the juniper and piñon bushes which lined the narrow road leading to the river. He then crossed the bridge in silence, passed the porch and walked directly to the garden behind the house. He could see Kate standing in the kitchen. Henry's light was off. Asleep, Ben hoped. He scooped up the cold black soil, smelled it and felt it seep between his fingers. There was no moon or stars, they had crept behind a bank of clouds which drifted down from Colorado. He rubbed the twenty dollar bill between his fingers, and thought of what it could buy him. Suddenly, the coyote howled again. Ben envied the animal. At least it let the world know how it felt.

The wind increased and whipped through the garden. Ben snapped up the collar of his jacket then touched the silver cross and chain around his neck. His mind reached back and he saw Two Crows stoop to lift him from the river, then the fire blazing in the tepee, and the meadow filled with flowers. Next, he pictured Nando working in the greenhouse and he thought of Luther, probably at home, laughing with his family, sharing fry bread on the porch. His eyes filled with tears. He turned his face to heaven to find the moon and stars he knew were there, but hidden by clouds which raced across the valley.

Suddenly, he heard the gate open and close. He froze. "Who's there?" As Ben slowly turned, the coyote howled through the darkness. He heard footsteps move toward him. "Who's there?" he asked cautiously. The footsteps seemed to circle him. He turned to follow the sounds, but only saw the hard, black dirt beneath his boots.

"Ben?" said the young voice.

He whirled around. His heart beat faster.

"Ben, can you see me?"

Enveloped by fear and blackness, Ben started to run toward the gate. "Don't go, Ben."

"Who's there? Show your face," Ben shouted as he stumbled to the ground.

"Here I am," she said softly. He looked up into the young girl's face, painted blue and yellow, glowing in the dark. A feather was tucked behind her ear. Her small fingers reached toward him. His mind raced back to the child he'd seen in the plaza and he continued to stare as he struggled to his feet. "How do you know my name? Weren't you at the dances today?"

"That's right. I watched you for a long time after the dancers had finished. You looked lonely Ben, sitting by yourself as the people left. I followed you home."

"Are you from Tesuque?"

"Yes," she answered.

"What's your name?"

"Agoyo."

"Never heard of it."

"You're sad now, aren't you Ben?"

"Why are you asking me such things? I've never seen you before today."

"Luther wants to see you. Go to his house in the morning. He'll be waiting on the porch."

Ben stared blankly at the small painted face and green eyes shimmering in the darkness.

"But now, go inside and give your mother the money in your pocket. That wasn't intended for you to spend on yourself. It's for your family."

Ben stepped backwards in shock. His jaw dropped as he listened in disbelief to the child who drew closer.

"Tell Kate you love her. She's sad tonight too, Ben. She needs love as much as you do, maybe more."

Ben looked away, then silence fell in the cold night air. The wind softened to a murmur. He turned in all directions, but she had vanished. Suddenly, the clouds broke and moonlight flooded the garden, the house and even the hills above the pueblo. The Milky Way sparkled, then Polaris emerged and seemed brighter than the sun.

Ben moved slowly toward the house but paused to watch the stars which now glistened like sapphires. He crossed the porch and found Kate at the kitchen table sipping tea.

"How were the dances, son?" she asked in a distant voice.

"O.K."

"That's all? Just O.K.?"

"There's something I want to give you." Ben reached out and dropped the money beside her teacup. "It's from Father Ortiz. Said to tell you he'd come by Sunday after Mass." Ben paused. "There's something else."

"Yes, son?"

"I want to say. . . I love you."

Ben watched moisture form in Kate's eyes as she touched his face and smiled. "I needed that," she said as Ben stood and walked toward his room, then paused.

"Mom?"

"Yes?"

"What does Agoyo mean in Tewa?"

"Star," was all she said.

Ben closed the door, and that night dreamed of things he'd never dreamed before.

SIX

Wake up boys, it's Christmas Eve. Amelia will be here any
minute," Kate said in a loud voice from the hall.

Henry rubbed his eyes. He was relieved that this year they
wouldn't make the pilgrimage to Chimayo. The year before, he remembered, he'd almost frozen to death. Ben yawned and watched the snow
float past his window. Kate tied the scarf around her neck, then waited on
the porch for the headlights which would cross the bridge at any moment.
She knew Amelia Ocate was never late for anything.

"She's here. Bring your heavy coats. It's snowing," shouted Kate from
the driveway.

Ben and Henry's boots made holes in the snow as they trudged toward
the Chevrolet. Henry slammed the door as Amelia gunned the engine. The
exhaust pipe belched a gray haze as she pointed the car toward the highway. From the back, Ben glanced at the clock embedded in the dashboard.
The green digits glowed eleven. Plenty of time, he thought, before midnight Mass at the Cathedral.

Henry believed Kate's reason for not walking to Chimayo. Ben didn't
buy it. Cold and snow had never stopped her before. He knew very well it
was her heart.

Amelia and Kate talked softly in the front. Henry went back to sleep.
Ben stared out the window at the banks of brown sludge the plows had
cleared that morning and as the Chevrolet's headlights parted the snow-
flakes, they seemed like fireflies in his garden on a warm night in July.

"Can we still go up Canyon Road?" Ben asked.

"There's time," answered Kate. "I want you boys to see the farolitos
on the roofs and the bonfires in the streets. They'll be singing Christmas
carols everywhere. But first, we're stopping at the plaza."

Ben smiled as he tried to picture the things Kate had described to them the night before. How Santa Fe became magical at Christmas, especially when snow was draped across the valley.

Henry stirred and opened his eyes. The traffic slowed for the downtown exit and soon they were huddled beside the obelisk in the center of the plaza. Piñon fires crackled, surrounded by people in heavy coats singing carols. The benches, usually filled with locals staring back at tourists, were vacant except for snow which rested on the hard, iron slats. Above, crooked branches draped in lights reached toward the low, gray clouds. Farolitos were everywhere: paper sacks filled with sand and candles, glowing warm and yellow in the snow which continued to fall as Kate, Ben, Henry and Amelia made their way from the plaza toward Canyon Road.

"Button your coats, it's freezing. We'll stay fifteen minutes," announced Kate through the thick wool scarf. Her breathing was heavy as they crossed Paseo de Peralta, then angled through the crowd which spilled into the street.

Pungent luminaria fires, built with piñon, guided them higher up Canyon Road past homes and walls crowned with farolitos. A family huddled around a luminaria singing "Silent Night" while the words drifted up in the cold night air to mingle with the embers.

As Kate's breathing became heavier, she paused halfway up the incline. Ben drew up beside her. "We don't have to go further. Let's walk back down to the cathedral. Anyway, midnight Mass is about to start," said Ben as he studied Kate's strained expression in the glow of a luminaria.

"I want to stay. I've only heard one Christmas carol," snapped Henry, his face buried in the hooded parka.

Kate steadied herself. Her breathing eased as they lingered by the fire. "Ben's right, let's go back down. We want good seats for Mass," said Kate as they began to move slowly through the crowd. Some held candles, others sang, but all seemed at peace in the spirit of Christmas Eve.

By the time they'd crossed Paseo de Peralta the snow had stopped. They paused on Water Street, as Saint Francis Cathedral loomed before them, the granite walls appearing like a fortress for believers who scurried up the steps. The church was almost full. Kate genuflected and led them to a pew midway down the aisle. Ben knelt between Kate and Henry, Amelia took the end seat by the aisle. A lone violin played "O Come Emmanuel" from a small room near the entrance. Ben crossed himself and studied the cavernous church; massive columns supporting the barrel vaulted ceiling, which led his eye to the white plastered dome above the altar. On the wall behind the altar hung the figure of Christ, dying on the cross. It reminded Ben of the crucifix in the chapel at Tesuque, only larger and more lifelike. Painted drops of blood trickled from a wound below the rib cage. A crown of thorns was jammed into the head, bent down from the agony which filled the tortured face. Crimson stains filled the pockets of the hands, pierced by nails. The organ blended with the violin and soon the church resounded with the voices of the choir.

Ben leaned to Henry and whispered, "The bodies of the bishops are buried under the altar." Henry shook his head in disbelief. "It's true," said Ben, "Father Ortiz said so. Ask Mother." Kate nodded in agreement as the bell rang and five hundred people stood as the clergy, dressed in long white robes, filed past, moving slowly up the aisle toward the altar. Ben inhaled the pungent incense spiraling up to the ceiling, a hundred feet above the priests, deacons and altar boys who sang louder than the choir. At the end of the procession, Ben saw the feeble looking man and his pointed hat which curved toward the ceiling. His gold embroidered vestments swayed with the music as he moved past Ben. Ben noticed that the walking stick he carried was taller than the hat. Then his eyes fell on the large, gold cross which dangled from his neck.

"It's the Bishop," Ben whispered to Henry who shrugged and cut his eyes to a young girl across the aisle.

"I've got to pee," said Henry loud enough for Kate and several other people to hear. Ben rolled his eyes. Kate leaned and said, "You can hold it Henry."

"No I can't."

Kate leaned over and said in a hushed voice, "Use the toilets behind the church. You have to walk outside, then follow the sidewalk to the back. Get back here as soon as you can. You'll miss the Gospel."

Henry made his way quickly down the aisle and out the door.

After twenty minutes, the Bishop approached the pulpit for the reading of the Gospel. Kate glanced at her watch as the rosary beads moved slowly through her fingers. Ben craned his neck toward the door. Amelia looked at Kate who loosened the wool scarf, then shot a worried glance to Ben. At the end of the homily, Kate began to breath heavily. Ben knew she was concerned. After what had happened at the Indian School, she had reason to be, he thought, as he stole another glance toward the door. Another twenty minutes passed before the Bishop raised the Host for everyone to see. It was time for communion as Kate leaned and asked anxiously, "Where's Henry? It couldn't have taken this long."

"He's in back. Probably felt embarrassed. We'll find him after Mass," replied Ben in a reassuring tone.

Later, the congregation filed slowly down the aisle and out into the frigid darkness. Kate, Ben and Amelia gathered at the bottom of the steps and scanned the crowd. Ben walked to the rear of the church, checked the restrooms, then quickly searched the parking lot. Amelia moved down Water Street peering into empty doorways. Kate remained on the steps, the rosary clutched between her fingers, her anxious eyes shifting between children who darted in and out of shadows.

An hour passed. By now Kate, Ben and Amelia had scoured the empty plaza and deserted side streets which led into the square.

"Henry!" shouted Ben, his voice echoing off the frozen snow which cracked beneath his boots. "Henry?" he shouted again, but there was no reply from the brooding silence of the plaza.

Suddenly, the lights strung across the trees went out. The piñon fires which blazed so brightly earlier, now smoldered in the darkness.

Ben crossed the plaza toward Kate, standing alone on the corner, her face twisted in fear.

"Oh God, Ben! What do we do? It's been two hours. God, I can't take this," she sobbed as fresh snow drifted through the black, gnarled branches. Kate watched Amelia come slowly toward them up San Francisco Street, her head lowered to the sidewalk. She knew Amelia hadn't found him.

"The police. There's a pay phone at the corner," said Ben as he hurried up the slippery sidewalk past the darkened windows of shops which lined the empty square.

Ben returned several minutes later. "I told them what happened. I gave Henry's description and Amelia's number to call. They're putting out a bulletin and said for us to go back home. They'll call as soon as they hear something."

Kate, shaken, dropped the rosary in her purse. Ben and Amelia walked on either side of her toward the car.

By morning, the snow had passed. Kate peeled bananas by the sink while a cold wind seeped from under the kitchen door. She was grateful for the sun which splashed across the counter and lit the nylon stockings filled with candy. She looked across the room at the juniper bush propped against the wall, its limbs dotted with aluminum foil she'd fashioned into balls.

Red and yellow candles secured with string hung from a single strand of lights which flickered on and off.

Kate turned and set the plate of sliced bananas beside the packages she'd wrapped the week before. Ben was to receive a sweater she'd bought with money Father Ortiz had given her. She lifted Henry's gift and felt the soft cap and gloves through the wrapping paper.

"Any word?" asked Ben as he moved from the hall toward the table.

"Nothing. I was awake all night."

"Me too."

"Last Christmas it was Ojo. This year Henry's gone. Will it ever end?" asked Kate who turned away from Ben to hide her strained face.

"They'll find Henry. Just wait and see, mother. I prayed real hard last night."

"I did too. Blessed Mother will protect him," she said wearily, then turned to the sound of tires in the driveway.

"It's the police. Oh God, they've come to tell us something awful," she said as she rushed down the steps toward the squad car.

"Are you Kate Touchstone?" asked the thickset, dark complected officer who slammed his door and peered at her through the gray lenses of his sunglasses. She quickly nodded without a reply. "Help me with your son. He's in the back seat."

Kate rushed past the man, then stood motionless as she stared through the window at Henry, curled in a ball, his head propped against the door. Henry stirred when cold air rushed into his lungs. Kate leaned over and smelled the wine which covered his clothing with small red circles.

"Is he?"

"Drunk, ma'am. Found him in the bushes behind Saint Francis Cathedral at three o'clock this morning. Another boy was with him. My partner chased him but he got away. How old's your boy?"

"Thirteen."

"Way too young to be drinking. This happen often?"

"Lately, yes."

"Let's get him inside. I need to finish my report."

"Report?"

"Yes ma'am. Got to write him up."

Kate felt her heart plunge to the bottom of her stomach. "He's only thirteen."

76

"That's the problem," he countered while reaching for a black book he took from the belt which held in check a bulging stomach. "Underage and intoxicated in a public place. He also resisted arrest. Maybe teach him a lesson. Got to do it ma'am," said the officer as he bent and lifted Henry from the seat. He then followed Ben down the hall to Henry's room.

Kate sat alone and watched the squad car back down the drive then lurch toward the highway. She stared at the yellow slip of paper. Henry's name, age and address were printed at the top. Next the date and what took place the night before in the shadows of the cathedral. She closed her eyes and thought of Ben. It was, after all, Christmas! Father Ortiz had told her he was dropping by to visit after the Christmas Mass he was offering at the pueblo. She had pork tamales in the freezer. Tea could be brewed in the sun which splashed through the gnarled tree above the porch. She'd stored flour and sugar in the pantry to make biscochitos cookies. Kate stood, her head erect, as her gray eyes swept the valley and the thin ice which floated on the river. Whatever it took to have a decent Christmas, she would do it. Then she thought of other families who had it harder than the Touchstones as she moved toward the pantry. She knew she still had Ben and Henry and her faith which had seen her through much darker days than this.

Amelia arrived within the hour, bringing presents for the boys and a sweater for Kate who had finished baking cookies. The tea was steeped and steamed tamales rested on the table. Soon Father Ortiz arrived and took his place at the far end of the table. The tiny strand of lights blinked in the corner to remind them it was Christmas.

Before they ate, they bent their heads. Ben felt a warmth run through him as Father Ortiz led them in a simple prayer, thanking God for everything which He had given. Kate said a special prayer for Henry, unconscious in his room.

SEVEN

Four years later spring erupted with a rush of water which surged down the dry arroyos and then twisted through the valley. Snow still clung to the mountains above the house and even on the cedars which flanked the gate in the garden. The days lengthened. Rabbits and chipmunks appeared, liberated from their burrows in the hills and warmed by winds which swept up from the south. A month before, farmers had tilled the land into patches forming quilts across the valley. Now it was time to plant the shriveled seeds from which the Española chile would spring.

Ben's feet hung limp over the end of the bed, his six foot frame had overtaken the remaining length of mattress. He stretched and felt the power in his arms and chest. His muscles were firm from running and from nights in the weight room after school. Comments from classmates concerning his Anglo features had subsided. He presumed his size and assumed strength had been the cause.

The early light fell across his face, now hard and chiseled, and as he shifted, he felt Two Crow's silver cross and chain slide across his chest. His striking features had brought interest from the girls in his classes. Especially Pilar Ocate, Amelia's daughter, who by anyone's standards was considered the catch among the senior class. Born in the pueblo, her skin was dark, the color of almonds. Her lean, curved body drew gapes from the boys as they huddled at the bottom of the stairs, yearning for a glance beneath her skirt. But she'd singled out Ben for attention. Maybe, he thought, because he had the look of an Anglo, or possibly it was his body which he stretched again before he pulled the pillow tight against his face to block the sun.

He recalled she'd lingered in the parking lot after class the week before as if to signal she was unattached. Her scent drew him closer as he stared at the deep, supple cleavage of her breasts. She smiled and said she'd meet him later behind the water tank, high on the hill above the pueblo. But why hadn't he pursued her? he wondered. At least ask her out? Ben couldn't explain it but knew there was something which kept him at a distance. A feeling, as if a seventh sense had ordered him to do so. Possibly, it was just her reputation, he thought, as he rolled onto his flat belly and considered the hard cracked dirt in the garden behind the house. He knew it should be planted, but there was time, he thought, then recalled once when Ojo had waited until now, and besides, he mused, it was such a tiny slice of ground.

At that moment, for the first time in months, he thought of the angel. Why hadn't she returned? Had she forgotten him? Nonetheless, Ben sensed the peace she'd left with him that night in the chapel. Every thought, every kind gesture toward his family, even strangers, had become important, as if each were drops of liquid silver, gifts which the angel had left inside his heart.

"Ben?" Kate called from the kitchen. "You awake? It's almost nine. Get up, you'll sleep your life away."

Without answering, he pushed the straw colored hair off his face, pulled on the jeans he'd dropped beside the bed the night before and walked slowly down the hall toward the kitchen.

"Here's your coffee," said Kate. "Father Ortiz called last night while you were out. Said he's having trouble finding money for us but reminded me school would be out soon. Maybe you and Henry can find some work?"

"Henry doesn't want to work. Haven't you noticed, he's hardly ever here."

"I know, I know. He's been. . . ."

". . . Staying out all night, mother. He's probably gone. Have you checked?"

"He's not back yet. It's the people he hangs out with, the low riders from Española."

"No, he hangs out with their younger brothers. I've seen them on the plaza in Santa Fe," added Ben as he dropped a spoon into the coffee cup.

"He wants to buy a car and join a car club," said Kate with disgust as she wiped her hands and pointed to the bowl of oatmeal beside his elbow.

"He's seventeen. He can't buy a car."

"He said he'd steal one if he has to." Kate released a sigh as she sat at the table with her coffee.

"I'll talk to him, mother." Suddenly they heard a car door slam and saw Henry listing at an angle, braced against the window of the Chevrolet.

"He's drunk, Ben."

"Stay here, I'll handle this," Ben said as he pushed open the screen door and walked toward Henry and two other boys seated in the low slung car. "Get inside Henry, mother's seen you. I can smell you from here," snapped Ben as he stared through the tinted windows at Henry's friends, quarts of beer clinched between their fists.

"Mind your own damn business, brother. Go into town and hang out with the honkies. Go on, Ben, those white skinned bastards love you."

"Shut up Henry and get inside. You make a scene out here and I'll kick your ass from here to Taos." Henry saw the veins in his brother's neck throb as Ben's fingers curled into fists.

"You want to try?" shouted Henry.

Ben swallowed hard. Henry watched Ben's eyes grow large. Ben knew he'd never come this close to confronting Henry. Suddenly, he saw the chrome barrel of a pistol pointed at him through the open window. Startled, Ben yanked the knife from his pocket and locked the blade. Henry shouted something to his friends as Ben moved toward the car. He watched Henry from the corner of his eye, then saw a thumb cock the hammer of the pistol.

Suddenly a flash of silver light electrified the air and a deafening clap of thunder shook the ground. Dark clouds had moved across the sun and blotted it from the sky. Fierce wind now drove across the field ripping leaves from trees. A limb above the car snapped and fell beside Henry, who covered his face as rain descended with fury, pounding their skin like buckshot. Ben staggered back and dropped the knife. The pistol vanished behind the window, quickly closed against the raging storm.

Suddenly, Ben heard the roar of the engine. In the grayness of the fury, headlights blazed into his face as the car backed wildly down the driveway toward the road which had become a river.

Ben stared at Henry through the violent rain. He saw him stagger, then drop to his knees, his hands shielding his face. Ben heard Henry call his name through the savage wind which tore at his clothes as he made his way to Henry, kneeling in the mud. Ben's strong hands gripped Henry's shoulders and pulled him up. He smelled the wine and heard his brother sobbing as they stumbled up the steps toward the kitchen.

A week later while seated on the porch, Kate gazed across the parched arroyos toward the pueblo and the hills, flecked with juniper and cedar then shifted her attention to the dirt road rising toward the highway. The barbed wire fence, which stretched the length of the road, steered her eyes to a figure which seemed to be running either toward the house or the bridge leading to the pueblo. She recognized the blonde hair which reminded her of wind blown wheat. As Ben neared the porch he quickened his pace.

"Good news," said Ben between gasps. Henry was leaning against the door frame, a toothpick dangling from his lips.

Ben collected himself before he continued, "Saw an ad in the paper this morning."

"And?" said Kate from the stiff wooden chair.

"There's a man up on Circle Drive in Santa Fe who needs a gardener. Just called him from the store. He said to come and talk."

"Wonderful!" exclaimed Kate. "I'm so proud of you." Henry shrugged.

"I hope I get the job," said Ben as he glanced at Henry, who shook his head and turned his attention to the slats beneath his pointed boots.

"But only for the summer, Ben. You're about to graduate. You need to think about a real job."

"I know," said Ben while staring at Henry.

"Henry's going down to Agua Fria tomorrow to see a farmer about some work, aren't you Henry?" Henry nodded then shifted the toothpick in his mouth. "You'll find work, Henry, the Lord will help you," Kate declared with enthusiam. Henry rolled his eyes, then walked slowly down the drive toward the river. As he walked, he thought how much he hated Ben. What Kate had said, "I'm so proud of you," rattled through his mind over and over until he'd distanced himself a quarter mile from the house and family he'd come to detest.

Reaching the bridge, he gazed down at the river. At that moment, he vowed to bring his brother down, no matter what it took.

EIGHT

Baxter Sneed leaned against the counter, smoothed his few remaining strands of silver hair then dropped the lime into the gin and tonic. He stared out at the range of mountains which flanked the Española valley and the hills below, sprinkled with piñon and juniper and considered once again if he should retire. He recalled the high risk deals he'd put together. To drill for oil where no one expected it. Baxter knew he still had quite a bit of clout and with the stock in his company, plus real estate investments, he knew he'd never have to work again. The oil company which bore his name had flourished and the offices, including the latest in Albuquerque, ran like the innards of a fine Swiss watch. If he ever decided to return full time, it would be an easy thing to do.

He continued to gaze out the kitchen window at his expanse of property, then up to the azure sky which stretched forever. On a clear day with binoculars he could see the mountains which circled Taos and every evening from the portal, he and Morgan watched the sun drop behind Los Alamos, its laboratories concealed within the mountain.

His mind reached back to Lydia, his wife of thirty years, and the cancer which had ravaged her body. Quickly he shifted his thoughts to Morgan, almost thirty years younger than himself and considered the joy she'd brought him during their first year of marriage. There was much talk in Dallas about his sudden marriage after Lydia's death which Baxter ignored and continued with his plans to marry Morgan even though, so the tongues wagged, she was young enough to be his daughter.

"Yes, I placed the ad. Who's this?" he asked bluntly while propping the receiver against his thin, wrinkled neck.

"Ben Touchstone. I talked to you yesterday."

"Can you come around four?" asked Baxter in a flat voice.

"I'll be there," replied Ben from the phone booth behind the store near the pueblo.

"Who was that?" asked Morgan standing on the lawn, her blonde streaked hair ruffled by a breeze.

"A boy from Tesuque named Touchstone. He's coming at four. I'd like you to be here Morgan," said Baxter while pulling on the worn cashmere sweater.

Morgan dropped a straw hat over her tanned, sculptured face and studied the Sangre de Cristo mountains to the east and the clumps of piñons, junipers and cedars scattered across the thirty acre estate on Circle Drive. "Baxter, I want a garden over there." She paused to adjust the dark sunglasses which covered her emerald colored eyes. "A flower garden," she continued, "a big one beyond those piñons where we'd see it every day. And another, carved out around the pool. Is he Mexican?"

"Who?"

"The boy that's coming."

"Maybe Indian, how the hell do I know? I really don't care as long as he can work."

"True. I just wondered with a name like Touchstone you can never really tell."

"I'd say Indian. Said he lives up on the edge of Tesuque. Barbara and Toby, are they still coming for dinner tonight?"

"Yes. I saw them at the market this morning. But they won't stay late. Toby's got business in Dallas tomorrow afternoon," said Morgan as she exhaled, then crushed the cigarette in the soil beneath her shoe.

Ben closed the door of the phone booth behind the store, zipped up his windbreaker and thought of what he would say to the people who lived on the ridge which overlooked his village. He knew they existed in a different world, a world he couldn't relate to, but only imagined after accounts from Ojo, who'd gardened for other wealthy families in Santa Fe. But he remembered what Kate had told him that morning, "Just be yourself. If God means for you to have this job, you'll get it."

Ben quickly crossed over the culvert in the dry arroyo and retraced his steps down the dust filled road which led to the bridge spanning the river. He felt he should change, but wondered what he would change into? Maybe a nicer shirt? He knew there weren't many other choices, but the t-shirt he was wearing would never do. Should he wear his only pair of good pants? Maybe not. If the man liked him, he might be put to work. No, he decided as he neared the house, he'd brush his hair and wear exactly what he had on. Like Kate said, just be himself.

An hour later Ben thrust his thumb in the air beside the highway which wove through the villages and pueblos scattered between Santa Fe and Taos. Within minutes he was in the rear of the truck, the wind against his face as he strained to see the ridge, and hopefully the house on Circle Drive perched above the valley. The outdoor opera house swept by and next the flea market with its canvas tents which leaned against the wind. Ben pounded on the window of the pickup, thanked the driver, and minutes later glanced up at the green tiles embedded in the tall stucco column which read: 561 Circle Drive. Ben studied the carved wood gate and the smooth adobe wall which curved from view before he pushed the button beneath the tiles. He imagined the walls of his own house were once this smooth. From behind a piñon tree, a man's voice crackled through the speaker.

"Who's there?"

"Ben Touchstone, I've come to talk."

"Wait, I'll be there in a minute," said Baxter from the kitchen as he reached for his loafers and called Morgan to meet him in the driveway.

Ben leaned closer to the gate and through a crack, studied the sprawling house, territorial in style, an endless mass of adobe connected by a bright tin roof. He thought there must be at least twelve rooms. There were footsteps and the sound of a latch being thrown. The gate opened and Ben stared back at the tall, silver-haired man, who inspected Ben with the shrewdness of a cattle trader.

"You're on time," said Baxter as he closed and locked the gate. Ben glanced at the woman standing in the driveway beside Baxter as she shielded her green eyes against the sun which defined Ben's rugged squared-off features, fair skin and straw colored hair. Ben guessed her age at thirty, maybe younger, and thought she looked young enough to be the daughter of the man who said in a deep voice, "I'm Baxter Sneed. This is Morgan, my wife. Follow us, I'll show you what we need done."

Within the walls, Ben scanned the enormous courtyard. His boots were enveloped by clover and overhead, the trellis, draped with twisted vines, blocked the sun. He followed them down the smooth gray flagstones which led into the zaguan, the Spanish-styled entryway which divided the public areas of the house from the living quarters.

"So you're from around here?" asked Baxter as they walked through the zaguan and out onto the portal with its broad view of the mountains and the valley. The pungent aroma of burning piñon streamed from a fireplace at the far end of the portal which seemed to be a hundred feet away. He noticed a hammock slung between two of the dozen white posts supporting the tin roof which jutted out to cover the porch. The floorboards, laid side by side and pointing north, disappeared around the corner. Baxter repeated the question as Ben returned his attention to the tall, thin man who leaned against the railing.

"I was born near Tesuque." Silence followed Ben's comment as Morgan glanced at Baxter while stepping off the portal onto lime green grass. Beyond the grass, piñon and juniper trees flowed down toward the valley.

"Touchstone. That's your family's name?" asked Morgan as she studied his extraordinary features, dulled by the shade of the portal.

"Yes."

"Have you done this kind of work before?" asked Baxter.

"My father, Ojo, did some gardening, then passed it on to me."

"And what about your mother? Is she from around here?" Morgan asked, probing further.

"She's from Hatch. She met Ojo when they worked together picking chilies for her father."

"Oh, I see," said Morgan as she looked away blankly, lit a cigarette and moved further down the steps toward the pool.

"Have you held a job before?" asked Baxter as he followed Morgan, a foot shorter than himself, who led the procession down the flagstones. Before Ben could reply, she stopped at the bottom, swung her lean, suntanned arm and pointed to the swimming pool. "This is where I want some flower beds. There, on either side of the pool, then down toward the trees. It's quite steep, can you do it?" As she spoke, Ben glimpsed an enormous diamond on her finger, then replied, "If the dirt's shored up with beams at the bottom—that will keep the soil from running off." Morgan nodded in agreement, turned and pointed to a clearing a hundred feet away between the junipers and the piñons at the opposite end of the portal. "And another garden, much larger, over there. We could see it from the kitchen. It would be lovely, don't you think?"

"I guess, but the soil's bad," said Ben.

"Bad?"

"Old and hard. Need to dig it out, then turn in mulch," he added.

"Can you furnish references?" asked Baxter as he trailed behind his wife.

"I suppose, from my school in Santa Clara. Mrs. Sanchez would vouch for me."

"Anyone else?"

Ben paused and recalled Nando, then thought of the old priest at Chimayo. "Father Ortiz, the priest at the church in Chimayo. He knows me, he's given us money before, when the chile crop failed or when. . . ."

"When what?" asked Morgan sharply.

"After my father left us."

"Oh? Why was that?" inquired Morgan, her eyes fastened on Ben, who now was flanked by the couple.

"When do you finish school?" Baxter interrupted before Morgan could continue.

"In a couple of weeks, then I graduate."

"Can you work through the summer?" Baxter asked.

"Sure."

"About your pay," said Baxter now leveling his hazel eyes on Ben who continued to inspect the clearing between the trees. "Let's say ninety a week."

"Seven days a week?" asked Ben, who stepped back to face Baxter and Morgan.

"Six, with Sundays off," snapped Baxter impatiently.

"A hundred fifty," Ben shot back.

"A hundred twenty five," Baxter countered in his deepest voice.

"I'll take it. We need the money, but when I've finished with the gardens?" Ben let the question trail off as he stared at Morgan who remained silent beside her husband.

"There will be plenty for you to do, Ben," Morgan said as she fumbled with the sunglasses. "Keep the pool, trim bushes, potting flowers. And possibly some inside work—windows, waxing floors. We'll see," she added casually.

"How long has this priest known your family?" Baxter questioned, his voice rigid.

"Since I was born."

"I'll call him, then call you back. What's your number?"

Ben's eyes dropped before he quietly answered, "No phone. Can't afford one. Call Hernandez store near the pueblo. They'll find me."

That evening in his bedroom, Ben considered the extraordinary things he'd seen and heard on Circle Drive. He prayed that Father Ortiz would be there when Sneed called and wondered what the priest would say.

At nine o'clock, Ben stirred as Kate's voice drilled through the bedroom door. "Ben, there's been a call for you at the store. Get up, maybe it's the man on Circle Drive." Ben pulled on his jeans and socks, yawned and walked into the kitchen.

"He left this number. Come right back. I want to know what he said." Ben stuffed the paper in the pocket of his windbreaker and walked quickly down the drive toward the store. Inside the phone booth he dialed the number.

"Yes?"

"It's Ben Touchstone."

"How about Saturday morning, say seven?"

"I'll be there. What did the priest say?"

"Enough for me to hire you."

"Tools? You've got tools?" asked Ben anxiously.

"Plenty. Just be ready to dig the beds. My wife's impatient," replied Baxter as he cradled the phone before reaching for his drink.

Ben replaced the receiver, stepped outside into the cool night air and smelled piñon, pungent like incense, burning in the house across the road. The moon seemed very bright—brighter, he thought, than it had been in quite some time.

He smiled, knowing for certain there was a God in heaven holding up the stars above Tesuque.

The following Saturday Ben mashed the button, then waited for a reply from the speaker hidden behind the piñon tree on Circle Drive. He pressed it again and through the cracks in the gate studied the small green car parked at the end of the driveway. The chrome, he thought, glistened like a silver concha belt. From the speaker came the voice of a woman, "Who is it?"

"Ben Touchstone."

"It's open. Come through the courtyard. I'm in the kitchen."

Ben walked down the drive through the courtyard then followed the slate stones through the heavy carved doors which led into the zaguan. A polished wood table filled the middle of the room. At its center, a crystal vase held long white gladiolus which reached toward the ceiling. He glanced to his left into the living room and saw the fireplace rimmed with gleaming marble and at the opposite end of the room bookcases, painted white, stretched from the hardwood floor up the adobe wall to the ceiling planked with large beams carved from cedar. He stared past the bookcases down a long hallway filled with plants and four open doors he assumed led to bedrooms. In the center of the living room was a white sofa flanked by matching wing-back chairs resting on an oriental rug which to Ben seemed larger than his house. Two vivid abstract paintings hung on opposite walls; the one to his left appeared to Ben like finger-paint, the one above the fireplace was even more baffling. Suddenly he heard her call his name. He turned and walked slowly past French doors and into the kitchen. Mrs. Sneed was standing by the window in the nightgown, her full, curved breasts outlined by the light. "Some orange juice, Ben?" Startled, his eyes shifted quickly from her to the polished tile floor then back again.

"Oh, no, I've eaten breakfast. It's—it's time I get to work," he stammered. "Is your husband here?"

Morgan's eyes began to track across his handsome face, down his chest to his thin, taut waist, when the sound of heavy boots abruptly switched her inspection of Ben to Baxter standing by the French doors. "Get dressed, Morgan," said Baxter in a sharp voice.

"I am dressed," she snapped. Morgan glared at Baxter, whirled and rushed from the room, her bare feet making slapping sounds on the tile floor. Baxter said in a hushed tone, "This is embarrassing."

"It's all right. She didn't do anything—just asked me to come into the kitchen. When I walked in. . . ."

"Yes, I know, I saw it all. Enough of that, let's go outside." Ben followed Baxter through the dutch door opening onto the portal, then down flagstones leading to the pool which to Ben seemed to be floating in the sky above the valley.

Minutes later Morgan reappeared as if nothing had happened. Dressed in jeans, a careworn sweater and sneakers, she motioned for Ben to follow her down the hill. "This is where I want the flower beds to start, then turn up toward the pool, and then I want a border of flowers by the decking. What will you need from the nursery?" she asked anxiously.

Ben walked down another ten feet and began to study the steep terrain before he replied, "Railroad ties and a dump truck full of mulch," he said while staring at the clearing at the opposite end of the portal.

"And flowers? I want lots of flowers planted," said Morgan from behind black lenses.

"Don't need them. Have them bring seeds. Cosmos, zinnias and daisy seeds."

Morgan glanced at Baxter who nodded, then made her way up the steps to the portal and into the kitchen.

"You just saved us quite a bit of money," said Baxter as he pointed to the shed behind the diving board. "The tiller's up there. I'll leave you to it. And Ben, let's forget about what happened in the kitchen."

"Fine with me," murmured Ben as he followed the concrete decking which hugged the border of the pool. As he walked toward the shed, he became aroused by the image of Mrs. Sneed standing in the kitchen: her lean, tanned body, the streaked blonde hair which framed her breasts and the look she'd given him before Mr. Sneed appeared in the doorway.

During the afternoon, Ben worked the hard clay soil with the tiller. All that remained was to place the beams at the bottom of the slope but that would have to wait for Monday.

From the portal, someone called his name. He straightened the tiller. It was Morgan staring at him. He leaned against the handles as a spherule of sweat made its way from his forehead down the side of his angular nose to his lips. He grimaced, then struggled up the incline with the ponderous machine.

Halfway up, she called his name again.

She approached slowly down the steps, her eyes scanning his sweat covered chest through the open shirt, then up to his proud, strong face, his prominent cheekbones and cobalt eyes.

"Sorry I embarrassed you," she said as she continued her study of his body. "I don't know what came over me. I guess I wanted to shock you."

"You did."

"I realize now it wasn't right—in my nightgown, knowing I'd see you in the kitchen. Let's forget about it?"

"Sure. Just surprised me, that's all."

"Then we're friends?"

"O.K. with me. Now I need to put this thing away and start back home. It's a ways back to Tesuque and the sun's going down."

"Let me drive you."

"I don't think. . . ."

"I'll grab my bag and meet you in the driveway." Before he could reply, she disappeared into the house. Moments later Ben stood quietly in the drive inspecting the wood and leather of the BMW. Morgan appeared, her streaked hair piled high above the tanned face, a cigarette protruding from coral painted lips. She motioned for Ben to open his door, then tossed a bag behind the seat. Ben, only inches from her shoulder, heard the engine roar, then grabbed the dashboard as Morgan spun the wheel leaving furrows in the gravel.

"You like it?"

Ben stared at the closed gate as the car gained speed. Morgan punched a button on the visor and the gate opened only seconds before the bumper cleared the entrance. "You like it?" she repeated as she glanced at Ben, his hand still braced against the dashboard.

"You almost hit the gate."

"Baxter gave it to me for my birthday."

"What?" gasped Ben, his eyes riveted on the curves which raced toward them.

"The car!" She slammed the shift into low as Ben watched the edge, only inches from the tires. "Grab a beer behind the seat," snapped Morgan as she shifted, then increased speed on the narrow road as it straightened from the hairpin turn.

"Beer?" said Ben in disbelief as he reached into the bag.

"Why not?" She braked hard for another sudden turn. Ben could see the sun, now a large orange ball, framed in the mirror as Morgan lifted the can of Coors from his hand and quickly pulled the tab.

"We've only been married a year. Baxter thinks I'm an angel. He can't say much. You should see him put the booze away at parties. This one's yours. Open one for me." Ben hesitated before he reached into the bottom of the bag.

The caustic flavor flowed past his tongue and down his throat. He sipped again as the warmth spread from his stomach to his chest.

"Ever had a beer?" Morgan asked.

"No. Tastes good, especially after working all day."

"Good, Ben, I'm glad you like it," she said, then slowed for the stop sign and the cars streaming into Santa Fe for the weekend.

"You live in Tesuque?"

"Yeah, just up the road."

She shifted hard from first to second, forcing Ben deep into the seat. She lit a cigarette and slowed to sixty.

Only the top half of the sun hovered above the Jemez mountains as the car accelerated through the lush valley sprinkled with farms, the vegetables arranged in meticulous rows. Ben sipped again. His head became lighter from the beer and the third cigarette Morgan had lit since they'd left the house. At a distance, the sky beyond the ridge deepened to purple as the last trace of color dropped behind the mountain.

"How many in your family, Ben?"

"Just me, my brother and my mother."

"Where's your father?" she asked while mashing a button to crack the window.

"He left us in the middle of the night," replied Ben, his voice trailing off as he stared out the window at the blackness.

"How terrible. Does your mother work?"

"No, the doctor says she shouldn't, because of her heart."

"Oh? And your brother?"

"He hangs out with guys from Española. A no good crowd. He's almost never home."

"So it's up to you?"

"Yeah, that's the way it's been since Ojo left, but we make out O.K. The Lord works things out."

"You believe in God?" Morgan asked with surprise as she quickly shifted gears.

"Yes I believe in God, don't you?"

"Let's say I haven't made up my mind. I've got awhile, don't you think Ben?" she asked, drawing hard on the cigarette.

"Don't you ever think about it?" Ben asked quietly.

"Never bring it up. Maybe around Christmas, but hardly any other time. I guess we're too busy. You know," she said bluntly, blowing smoke against the windshield.

"Turn left at the Billco Carpet sign. Follow the road to the store."

"I thought you lived in Tesuque?" asked Morgan.

"I do."

"Then I should turn right, at the village?"

"No. I live near the pueblo."

"Oh, I see. The pueblo. And where is that?"

"A little further. Turn left, like I said, at the Billco Carpet sign. Just leave me on the road."

"Why not take you home?" asked Morgan before she tossed the empty can behind the seat. "Can I ask you something Ben?"

"What?"

"Why don't you live in the village like everybody else? Why do you live near the pueblo?"

Ben dropped his head and stared at the carpet between his legs. She saw his hands tighten in the dull red glow of the instruments. "Did I say something wrong?"

"I'm what you call a half-breed. My mother's white, my father's a full blood. Guess you wanted to know since you first laid eyes on me?"

"Oh no Ben, I was just. . . ."

"Curious, like everybody else? That's O.K. I'm used to it. Just let me out here beside the road. I'll walk."

"Oh God, I've done it! I *was* curious, Ben. You're very handsome in a different way than I'm used to. I mean that as a compliment." She studied his profile and flaxen hair which hung limp, almost to his nose. "Like I said, let's be friends. I'd like to drive you home. It's cold."

Ben sighed, nodded, then pointed a hundred yards beyond the BMW as it eased down the hard, dirt road. As they neared, he motioned for her to continue further toward the river.

Morgan lit another cigarette, slowed the car to a crawl and followed his directions to the small adobe house surrounded by a field.

"This is it. Not much to see," Ben mumbled. He reached for the handle then felt her nails brush against his cheek.

"Ben, I'm sorry if I insulted you. Are we still friends?"

Ben looked away before he spoke. "I'll be there Monday."

A month later Ben leaned against the railing of the portal, examining at a distance the seedlings which had erupted the week before. He knew the zinnias would establish themselves as well as the cosmos, but the borders of daisies he wasn't sure of. Another dose of fertilizer, he thought, would probably save them. Then Morgan appeared, a notebook clutched in her hand.

"It's beautiful Ben. Even Baxter's surprised. But I think it's time to plant cactus between the flowers, don't you think?" Without turning, Ben shook his head.

"Don't you want a natural look?" he asked.

"Absolutely," replied Morgan who opened to the first blank page she could find.

"I think small piñon bushes would do fine."

"No cactus?" she said with surprise.

"They're not native to Santa Fe," Ben added dryly as he shifted his attention to the other crop of annuals which swept from the border of the pool, then down the hill to the wood beams he'd set in place the month before.

"And over there?" asked Morgan, pointing her long slender finger at the beds beyond the portal.

"The same, I think," said Ben assuredly. "Trust me. The less you plant, the better it will look."

"Less is more. Right Ben?"

"I guess," he answered as he glanced at Morgan scribbling in the notebook.

Ben walked to the end of the portal and paused at the flagstones leading to the pool. He looked across at the two arms of mountains embracing the valley and recalled how it felt when she'd touched his face, then remembered her curved body underneath the nightgown and the look she'd given him before she hurried from the kitchen.

"Ben!" shouted Baxter. Ben's head jerked toward the pump house. Moments later Ben was standing at the door, waiting for Baxter to straighten himself over the pipes which jutted from the filter. "Ben. We need to talk," he announced before dropping two blue tablets into the tank beside his elbow. "It's about Morgan."

Ben sucked in breath and replied in a cautious voice, "Yes?" then glanced down at the white hairs which curled into tiny balls on Baxter's chest.

"She's concerned...." Ben waited nervously for what he feared Baxter was about to say, "... about the party. I want the place to look as good as possible. We're having a lot of people over, important people. Call the nursery, order anything you want. I want things perfect. Understand?"

"Yes sir," replied Ben as he exhaled slowly, walked up the steps toward the portal and stopped to stare at the hills around Tesuque. He felt confused. He knew his life was changing but for the better or worse he wasn't sure. He thought of Kate, probably alone in the kitchen making dinner, and Henry, whatever he was doing. "The Lord will work things out," he recalled Kate saying. Then he thought of the angel and wished she'd come again.

The following Saturday, Ben settled into one of the iron benches which lined the sidewalks and studied the German shepherd chewing scraps beneath the obelisk in the center of the plaza. He heard a child laugh over the prattle of an old man hawking imitation turquoise. A gust blew leaves across the flagstones as Ben switched his attention to the tourists. Some perched on benches. Others were strolling and staring at the locals who stared back.

Ben felt grateful for the day off, the first in weeks, and he intended to make the most of it. He crossed his legs and stared again at the dog as it began a slow lope in his direction. He slowly reached into his pocket and felt the package of peanuts he'd bought that morning at Kaune's grocery. The dog looked lean, much too lean, Ben thought as he extended his hand toward the animal who eyed him with suspicion. Ben sat motionless as he studied the dog and the tourists in the plaza, sunning themselves on the first clear Saturday since the first week of July.

"Good dog," Ben said quietly as the dog began to lick his palm. The peanuts vanished and Ben stared down into the sad brown eyes. "Come with me," Ben said before he stood and angled across the plaza, then strolled down Washington Street past the shops filled with tourists.

As they walked, Ben remembered when he could have entered any shop in Santa Fe with his own dog. But that was years ago. Things had changed.

Recently, tourists had stayed on to become locals. They'd brought their own meaning of the word progress, which altered the old to fit the new. Ben recalled the plaza from years before. The small cafes, family run shops and the five and dime store where Ojo had bought him ice cream after they'd folded their table and walked up from the market. Only the old pueblo women sitting cross-legged on the sidewalks selling jewelry remained unchanged.

As they crossed the street, viga beams poking from the buildings threw pointed shadows on the sidewalk. Ben walked to Sena Plaza, the long row of shops jammed with tourists. He glanced back at the dog before rounding the corner, then waited for the shepherd to thread his way through the crowd which spilled into the street.

Ben sensed the people staring, especially the tourists, probably wondering just how much of an Indian he really was. But he recalled what Mrs. Sneed had said—that she found him handsome—so he shrugged, quickened his pace and passed the galleries and expensive shops he'd never entered. Ben stepped aside for a second wave of tourists who plodded past him and looked beyond the Cathedral to San Francisco Street. The tempting aroma of fried tortillas and chilies was heavy in the air and grew stronger as he neared the entrance to La Fonda Hotel. He waited for the dog to settle, then walked into the lobby.

Ben made his way across the polished stone floor, worn smooth from eighty years of traffic. Dressed in jeans, mud covered boots and denim shirt, his appearance drew stares as he stepped through the tall glass doors, painted blue, into the crowded restaurant. Three elderly ladies dressed in denim skirts, concha belts and flowered blouses, shot glances toward him then resumed their conversation. A middle aged woman glanced up. Her neck was wrapped in turquoise, an arm supported silver bracelets reaching almost to her elbow. She carefully studied Ben over the rim of her coffee cup. He looked away, then up to the tall ceiling hung with chandeliers suspended from a skylight. The din of clattering plates and idle conversations swirled around him. Waiters brushed by as if he was invisible. Ben felt uncomfortable and out of place. He walked quickly from the restaurant, crossed the lobby and out into the clear, warm air to where the shepherd was sleeping on the sidewalk.

Ben was hungry and getting more so every minute. He crossed a bridge which spanned a stream. Two blocks further he slowed at the brightly painted building. Pink Adobe Restaurant was scrawled across the stuccoed wall. He peered through the window at the low-walled booths carved from thick adobe, filled with people eating off polished metal plates. The food looked delicious. He glanced down at the dog standing beside him, then studied the menu posted by the entrance. He scanned the list of choices, most of which he'd never heard of. His eyes stopped at *Poulet Marengo*. Ben stepped back, then read the price: $15.25. He saw *Tournedos* printed at the bottom. The price read: $16.95. Ben blinked. He heard laughter coming from the restaurant. Smiling people lifted glasses of wine which sparkled from candles throwing shadows on the walls. Then he studied the bright colored paintings like the ones, he recalled, in the zaguan on Circle Drive. He turned from the menu and watched as the shepherd trotted across the bridge toward the plaza. He'd hitch a ride back to Tesuque, he thought, and make a sandwich in his kitchen.

The following morning Ben stared at the ceiling, its warp and woof of viga beams and latillas sealed with mud. His mind raced with thoughts of the previous afternoon. It was as if he'd been in another world. The hotel, the restaurants, the people and their clothes—it all spun through his mind until the sun began to slant against the wall beside his bed. He opened his eyes and watched the column of light creep slowly up his arm, then he heard Kate's slippers in the hallway and remembered it was Sunday morning.

"You awake son? Thought I heard you stir," she said through the door. "I've got something to tell you. Wake up."

"I'm awake. Is Henry here?"

"No, maybe he's gone to the store."

"I doubt it, but I'll get dressed."

Ben found Kate on the porch, smiling, with a letter in her hand. "Sit down Ben." She slowly opened the envelope, then handed it to Ben and said, "You have a scholarship to college." Ben stared in shock. "Your principal, Mrs. Sanchez came by while you were in town yesterday. She heard from the college. You start classes in September. Ben, you're going to college! Can you believe it?" exclaimed Kate.

Ben studied the letter signed by the provost of Saint John's College in Santa Fe. He read it twice, then grinned.

"No, I can't!" he said as he continued to read. "It says Father Ortiz also sent a letter recommending me."

"And your grades were good, Ben. Very good. They made the difference," said Kate who wiped tears from her eyes and leaned to hug Ben.

"I can't wait to tell Amelia. She's meeting us at the bridge before Mass. Get dressed, son," Kate declared with exuberance. "This is the most exciting thing!"

As they entered the plaza, the bell's clang rumbled through the cemetery, filled with rocks and wood crosses which leaned at odd angles above the graves. Ben dipped into the holy water font and stepped aside to hold the door, allowing Kate and Amelia to enter the sanctuary. He could only see backs of heads, some veiled, but most tilted to the crucifix behind the altar. He watched Father Ortiz who clutched the breviary between his thin, bony fingers, genuflect before the tabernacle then walk slowly to the confessional beside the altar. Ben crossed himself and made his way down the side aisle and into the small, cramped box.

"Bless me father. It's Ben Touchstone. I need to talk."

"Yes Ben, I spoke to the man who called."

"I know father. Thank you. And I've got even better news. I've been given a scholarship to Saint John's in Santa Fe. I start next fall. Thanks for your letter."

"I wanted to help."

"But I need to talk."

"What's wrong?" asked the elderly priest who leaned forward and draped the purple stole around his neck.

"I'm confused."

"About what?"

"About the world I'm seeing. It's full of things I never dreamed of."

"Like what?"

"Like big houses where people don't care if they spend a thousand dollars on their flowers. And restaurants where I couldn't even recognize the food. I'm feeling lost, father, like the world's passed me by."

"Go on."

"One day I walked into the kitchen and saw the woman I work for sorting clothes. She had a big pile on the floor. She said to throw them in the trash. They were nice clothes, father. I bundled them up and took them home for mother."

"That was good what you did. Some people in the world take for granted the gifts which God has given them. He wants us to share. It's sad Ben, but some people never think of others. But you did. Look what you did for Kate. She'll not forget that."

97

Ben glanced up at the brass crucifix above the lace curtain which shielded him from Father Ortiz, whose expression of concern had altered to compassion.

"I worry about her," said Ben as he leaned back slightly from the odor of stale perspiration embedded in the priest's vestments.

"I know you do. And she worries about you and Henry, how you both will make out in the world. Now that you've gotten a scholarship, try and keep the job you have. Work weekends. The money you make helps your family survive. Listen to me, Ben. Put your trust in God. He will never let you down. And be kind and forgiving to everyone, even to the woman who threw away the clothes. I've got to go. It's time for Mass."

"There's something else, father."

"What is it?"

"I saw an angel."

"You saw what?"

"I saw an angel at the church in Chimayo, in the room that holds the sacred soil. It was five years ago on Christmas Eve."

"Oh, I see," said the priest distantly, "we'll talk about it later. I have to go."

As Ben pushed open the door of the confessional, his eyes fell on Kate and Amelia kneeling in the pew, their faces bowed in prayer. He watched Father Ortiz walk past the altar and into the sacristy and thought of what the priest had said. He glanced sideways at Kate, her face buried in her hands. Ben touched her arm and smiled.

NINE

One week later Harry Northcutt's fingers seized the drain at the bottom of the pool. He watched bubbles escape through his puckered lips and float slowly to the surface. He'd hovered there for only ninety seconds, but to him it seemed forever. Motionless, he stared at the hot Texas sun, ablaze in July, its shape distorted by the twelve feet of water above his head. He struggled to conserve the last few centimeters of air in the bottom of his lungs. Pressure built within his ears. Oxygen depleted, he felt his heart pound. His face inflamed, he bent his knees and launched himself toward the surface. Harry had a beer riding on the outcome.

"You owe me, Matt," Harry gasped as he slumped into the lounger beneath the diving board filled with screaming children, poised like lemmings ready to hurl themselves into the air.

"No way, Northcutt. I timed you. Ninety seconds doesn't cut it," laughed Matt, propped in the lounger next to Harry.

"I'm shorter. That counts for something," said Harry.

"You're fatter," quipped Matt.

Harry frowned, then motioned to the waiter standing in the shade of an umbrella, a note pad in his hand. Harry pointed silently at the wet towel behind his neck. The waiter quickly removed it as Harry slid the Raybans to the end of his short, round nose. He glared up at the children, who shrieked as they leapt into the air.

"Monsters," he snapped and leaned forward to make room for the fresh towel the waiter draped across the backrest.

He knew this would probably be his last summer of total irresponsibility. The past year at Highland Park had been an endless round of placement tests and he was delighted it was finished. He was ready for Vanderbilt.

Whether it was ready for him really didn't concern Harry. He was a Northcutt and planned to have his way just like his father, no matter what.

"Awesome," mumbled Harry as he stared through his dark glasses at a girl spreading sun screen on her flat, tanned stomach. "Who is she, Matt?"

"Don't know," his friend replied, sipping from the can of cola.

"Probably from out of town," declared Harry who continued to stare.

"She's out of your league, Harry. Chicks like that don't go for short, fat guys. You should know that."

"She'll like my money," Harry grunted as he rolled onto his stomach, fat squeezed between the webbing of the lounger.

"That's disgusting, Harry. Is that all you think about?" snapped Matt who motioned to the waiter as he pointed to his empty can of cola.

"I'll have her buck naked in my Porsche by midnight," said Harry in his flat nasal twang.

"You're incredible," laughed Matt. "I've got to go. I'll call you later," he added as he signed his parents name to the charge slip which he tossed on the waiter's tray.

Harry didn't move for several minutes, pressed into the webbing, peering sideways at the girl across the pool. He wondered if Matt really meant what he said. He didn't think of himself as fat, a little chubby possibly, but fat, never! he mused before rolling on his back to fall asleep.

Twenty minutes later he was awakened by the same waiter who leaned and handed him the phone. "It's for you, Mr. Northcutt," he said quietly, his voice barely audible over the squeals of more anxious children on the diving board. Harry wiped sunscreen and sweat from his face and propped the phone against his shoulder. "Yesss?" he answered dramatically, stretching out the word for several seconds.

"Harry, are you sitting down?" asked his father from the living room of their home on Turtle Creek, a five minute drive from the Dallas Country Club.

"Lying down, actually. What is it?"

"You've been rejected by Vanderbilt."

The phone slid down his stomach and clattered on the tiles beneath the lounger. Stunned, he waited for several seconds before he reached for the phone and lowered his voice. "How can that be? My grades are fine."

"They're way below average," said his father.

"O.K., so they're not perfect. I thought you knew the provost?"

"I do Harry. The letter says your SAT scores aren't acceptable."

"Lots of my friends are going there. Everybody's going there! Don't you see how important this is? I mean. . . what will I do? I can't face them anymore, especially Matt. Something's got to be done. Don't you know anyone else at Vanderbilt?" he asked in a whisper.

"No, but I'll try. It doesn't look good, son. You need to come home now, your mother wants to see you."

"About what?" asked Harry, his words barely audible.

"Another school."

"What school?" Harry shot back, his tone rising with indignation.

"A small college in Santa Fe, Saint John's."

"Never heard of it."

"That's why she wants to talk to you. She has brochures. Come home, we're waiting."

Disgusted and angry, Harry switched off the phone and dropped it on his white, bulging stomach. He lifted his hand and waved a finger in the air above his head. The Hispanic waiter appeared and waited for the order.

"Bourbon. . . a double," he said sharply while staring directly ahead. The waiter paused to glance at Harry then cleared his throat. "But sir, I believe you're under age. . . ." He stopped in mid-sentence and stood motionless when Harry glared back, anger rising in his eyes. "Get me the damn drink or I'll have your brown ass shipped back to Mexico."

The waiter nodded quietly, turned and walked toward the bar, stopping only once to drape a towel across a lounger.

Thirty minutes later, Harry stood in the kitchen, his eyes riveted on his father. Stainless steel appliances filled the spacious room. Hand painted tiles bordered the cabinets which wrapped sixty feet around the island in the center. Above the island hung copper pots and pans gleaming in the sun which filtered from the skylight. Harry's eyes followed John's every move. Standing face to face, he studied his father: short and squatty with similar features as his own. But John's face was wrinkled and he was bald. He waited as John reached for the letter tucked in the pocket of his blazer.

"Like I said, you can't get in with these scores, son. That's all there is to it. I called and spoke to my friend at Vanderbilt. He'd like to help but there's nothing he can do."

Harry's mother entered quietly and glanced across the island at Harry who looked away.

"Margaret, I was telling Harry about. . . ."

"I know, I heard you from the living room," said Margaret, her hair dyed henna red was piled in a sweep above her plump, round face. "It's a shame, Harry. I know you expected to attend Vanderbilt but like your father said, there's nothing we can do."

Harry rolled his chocolate colored eyes helplessly and stared at the brick floor.

"There's an option," Margaret continued as she hefted her portly frame onto the stool. "John knows the provost of a small college in Santa Fe. He's already spoken with him. You've been accepted for the fall on one condition: good grades will be required and you must have a special tutor. One or two semesters, then you can transfer to Vanderbilt."

Harry's mind was numb. He wondered what his friends would think? Would they accept him when he transferred to Vanderbilt? He searched for a response but chose to remain silent as Margaret opened the brochure and pointed to the photographs.

"It's lovely there Harry. You'll have the mountains—and skiing and fishing if you'd like. I hear the students come from all across America. And just look at the campus. Simply beautiful!" she exclaimed, then waited for her son's response.

John stood quietly beside the sink. He knew exactly what Harry was thinking. He'd said many times they'd been cut from the same bolt of fabric. He was also aware they shared the same brutal instincts for survival which, he thought, was probably the reason they got along so well. John and Harry referred to it as tenacity. People who knew the Northcutts called it selfishness and greed.

The gossip around Dallas concerning the Northcutts was interminable, fueled by Margaret who took every opportunity to insure their faces habitually graced the social pages of the *Dallas Morning News*.

The social set whispered that John's oil and gas holdings were inherited from his father who'd struggled as a roughneck in Louisiana before discovering an oil patch north of Midland. The rumors spread that the elder Northcutt lied to local farmers then stole the leases, but nonetheless, he had made a fortune which he bequeathed to his son the day before he died. When the Northcutt name was whispered, it was usually coupled with Baxter Sneed. Five years before, Baxter attempted the most ruthless corporate takeover Dallas had ever witnessed. Tongues still wagged how personal it became and the articles which filled the *Dallas Morning News* were legendary. The most cherished was an article and photograph of John

Northcutt, dressed in only a towel, physically threatening Baxter Sneed with a six iron in the locker room. For Baxter's sake, the manager of the Dallas Country Club was forced to intervene. The year long battle became scandalous and some said was the reason Baxter sold his home in Dallas and moved to Santa Fe. Others disagreed, saying it was the painful memory of his wife's tragic death from cancer which drove him to the mountains.

Nonetheless, the new Junior League building bore the Northcutt name on the cornerstone. It was Margaret's legacy to insure perpetual adoration by the socialites of Dallas.

Harry walked across the kitchen, opened the refrigerator and removed a half-eaten sandwich he'd made the day before. "What kind of place is it?" he asked.

"A small, liberal arts school. A good foundation when you transfer to Vanderbilt," added Margaret who glanced at John who draped the blazer across his shoulder.

"Where will I live?" Harry asked through a mouthful of bologna and bread.

"In a dormitory, of course," replied Margaret with surprise.

"Are the dorms co-ed?" Harry asked while studying the last bite of sandwich.

"Certainly not. It's like Vanderbilt, only smaller," Margaret said in a reassuring manner.

"Nothing's like Vanderbilt, mother. You're just making it sound better than it is. I've never even heard of the place."

"There's a lot you haven't heard of Harry," snapped John. Harry plunged his large brown eyes to the floor as if on cue, which reminded John of their cocker spaniel who died the year before. Harry continued to chew the sandwich, then asked, "Didn't the Sneeds build a place in Santa Fe? I hear it's huge."

A touchy silence followed before John loosened his necktie and cleared his throat. "Harry, I told you never mention that name in this house. I've said it a hundred times," his words rising in anger. Margaret grimaced, then slowly raised her fingers to her throat to touch her pearls.

"Sneed," grunted John. "That son of a bitch came close to stealing everything I own. You know that don't you, Harry?" John shouted, as the veins in his neck began to throb. "Someday he'll screw up, and I'll find something that will ruin his ass forever," screamed John at the top of his voice.

Harry looked at Margaret who turned away as John wiped his mouth with his sleeve, before he added, "Apologize, Harry, for mentioning his name."

"I'm sorry I. . . ."

"Speak up son, I can't hear you."

"I'm sorry I mentioned his name," repeated Harry in a rigid voice while staring out the window, a shred of lettuce hanging from his lip.

John looked hard at Harry who continued to peer out the window. Margaret adjusted the pearls coiled around her baggy neck.

"It's not open to discussion, Harry," said his father bluntly. "If you want to go to Vanderbilt, this is the only way. You haven't much choice, do you son?"

Harry looked at John, then at Margaret who smiled back, her thick fingers clutching the brochure. "Only for one semester?" Harry asked.

"If your grades are perfect," John said as he turned to leave.

"If you insist, I'll go, but I want another car. Mine is almost five years old."

"That's fine son, anything you want," said Margaret, who smiled, then followed her husband down the long book-lined hallway.

Harry leaned against the counter, his almond eyes shooting holes through his parents as they disappeared into the living room. Hatred and resentment surged through him; hatred for his parents for what they'd decided, resentment of his friends he felt would abandon him. But he had his parents exactly where he wanted them. Now anything he wanted he would get. It would cost his parents dearly, he thought, but it would be a modest price to pay for his affection.

TEN

Ben sat alone on a bench beside the lily pond and watched students crisscross the courtyard, moving quickly between the low, modern buildings of the campus. From the waterfall which fed the pond, a breeze blew a fine mist across his face. He shifted on the bench and glanced down at the algebra book balanced on his knees. Positioned in the hills above Santa Fe, the sweeping views from the college were breathtaking.

After a month of classes, Ben had settled into the rhythm of his new surroundings. He shared a room with a boy named Gerald from Boston, who was pale, very thin and hardly spoke to anyone. Gerald ate by himself, went to class and studied late into the night. If he wasn't in his room, Gerald could be found in the library, hunched over piles of books, his round wire glasses propped at the end of a slim, straight nose. Ben had decided to find another roommate for the coming semester, at least one that would speak when spoken to.

A short time later, from his window, Ben stared out at the aspens which shimmered gold in the clear autumn light dappling the campus. It was then he noticed the low white sports car turn slowly into the parking lot. Chrome gleamed against the black rubber molding. The driver gunned the engine and Ben heard the growl, then music blaring from the speakers. He noticed how the black cloth top fitted snugly to the sloped curves which lent a sense of motion to the car. He looked closer and saw the short, stocky driver lock the door then walk through the parking lot toward the courtyard. Dressed in khaki slacks, polished loafers and red knit shirt, he moved with assurance as he greeted other students who passed him on the sidewalk. Ben saw the Texas plates and for a moment, imagined he owned the car himself.

He turned from the window and studied his clothes hanging in the closet: three pairs of jeans, two denim shirts, one pair of gray wool slacks, a parka, the sweater Kate had given him for Christmas and a white long sleeved shirt he hardly ever wore. He thought of the driver of the sports car and wondered if his clothes had helped to gain the friends he'd greeted on the sidewalk. But his mind wandered back to what Kate had said before he left, "Ben, just be yourself."

Later in the evening, Ben moved slowly through the serving line in the cafeteria with its tall glass windows which tendered lavish views of the mountains and the city. He thought briefly of the cafeteria at the Indian School, then pointed to the sirloin strip. Every meal had become a ritual, even breakfast, when he ordered pancakes and sausage with regularity. He handed the plastic food card to the woman by the register, then moved through the crowded room filled with students chatting over dinner, books stacked around their plates. He took his place alone in the corner, then saw the owner of the sports car turn and walk toward him, his polished loafers making clicking sounds as he approached.

"This booth taken?" he asked in a nasal twang.

"Help yourself," answered Ben while staring at the gold watch which dangled from his thick wrist.

"My name's Northcutt, Harry Northcutt. I'm from Dallas."

Ben looked across the table as Harry dropped his napkin to wave at a girl seated near the register. Harry began to eat without looking up. A minute passed.

"My name's Ben."

Harry finished the pasta then pushed away the plate. "Glad to meet you. Didn't catch the last name?"

"Touchstone. I'm from New Mexico."

"Indeed! A true native, huh?"

Ben paused for several seconds before he answered slowly, "Yes, a native."

"You must have connections or damn good grades to get in here," said Harry through a mouthful of salad. "Where you from?"

"Tesuque."

"I've heard of it. Lots of wealthy people retire there, in fact, friends of my parents have a house there. Got a polo field and horses. You may know them, the Stricklands from Dallas? They're up there all the time," remarked Harry while quickly consuming the ice cream sundae which ran down his lip.

Ben looked away and thought of what to say. "The name's not familiar. Are they locals?"

"Nope, but they spend half the year there playing polo. Ever tried it Ben?"

"What?"

"Polo."

"No, never, but. . . ."

"Exhilarating sport, but dangerous as hell. Old man Strickland was run down by a horse. Broke both arms and crushed his rib cage. Too damned dangerous for me. Give me a hot girl on a cold night and a bottle of rum. Now that's exciting! What d'ya say Ben?"

"Sounds great," replied Ben in a low voice as he pierced the apple pie, then glanced at Harry who smiled at a tall, thin girl, dressed in jeans and sweater who drew up to the booth.

"Beth, so good to see you. Missed you last night at the Pink. We had a fine time—closed the place down."

"I heard," said the girl, her slender face framed with hair the color of lemons. Ben turned and saw the large gold hoops which punched holes in her earlobes.

"I want you to meet Ben—Ben Touchstone. He's a native. Born and raised in Tesuque."

"Really? Tesuque?" said the girl in a rising tone. Ben nodded as she continued, "It's beautiful up there. I've stayed with friends who have a summer house there. They even have a polo field."

"You mean the Stricklands?" asked Harry. Ben's eyes darted between Beth and Harry.

"Do you know Cathy?"

"Know her parents. Her father plays golf with my dad."

"Ever seen their place in Tesuque?" asked Beth glancing quickly at Ben.

"Not yet," said Harry in an offhand way.

"A constant stream of friends, all summer long. A lot of Dallas people," said Beth as she tossed back her hair.

"Like who?"

"The Wilsons, the Pettigrews and the Sneeds."

Harry's eyes jerked toward Beth. His neck tensed. "The Sneeds of Dallas? The ones that have a house up here?"

"Sure."

"Their place is up on Circle Drive. I know them," said Ben casually, as he glanced at Beth and Harry for their reaction.

"Ben, you know the Sneeds?" questioned Harry in an anxious voice.

"Yeah, worked for them all summer. Practically lived with them. Now I work there on the weekends."

Stunned, Harry sat in silence for several seconds. The possibilities to help his father raced through his mind. Here was someone who was close to the Sneeds. Like Ben said, he practically lived with them. Harry knew if Ben was handled properly, he could contribute a wealth of private details. Overheard conversations between the Sneeds and deals put together on the telephone. Ben could gather a lot of dirt he thought, and he knew his father would reward him for it.

"Ben, is this your first year here?" Beth asked as she turned to face him.

"My first semester."

"How do you like it?" she asked, then glanced at his blue eyes and muscular arms which jutted from the denim shirt.

"Pretty well."

"Harry, we need to get together. Ben, you should join us sometime. A group of us go up to the ski basin and take picnics. . . ."

"That's not all we take," laughed Harry. "Beth's not telling you the full story."

"I've got to run. Nice to meet you Ben. Join us sometime." Beth smiled then quickly crossed the room toward the entrance. Harry waited until she passed the register before he spoke, "She's got the hots for you Ben, I can tell."

"What?" said Ben as he folded his napkin.

"I saw her staring at you. Didn't you notice?"

"Nope."

"Ben, she'd be good in bed, her long legs wrapped around you like a python. You ought to ask her out."

Ben stared at Harry who smiled then nodded to another girl, this one a brunette who settled at a nearby table. "Do you know the whole school?" Ben asked.

"No Ben, just the ones that count. I call it social politics. Some people count, some don't. The ones that can help me network in the circles I want to travel in I'll get close to. The others aren't worth my time. And Beth, I'd love to lay her, but her parents know my parents. See them all the time at parties in Dallas. Her dad does deals with my dad. Too close to home. Might muddy the waters for me, don't you see?"

"Yeah, I think," said Ben as he chewed on ice he'd sucked up from his water glass.

"And besides, there's a whole lot of women up here I'd like to meet. If word gets out I'm only seeing Beth, I'd be dead meat to all the other girls. You've got to think about these things."

"Yeah, I suppose. Harry, can I ask you something?"

"Sure."

"Is that your white sports car parked outside?"

"Absolutely. You saw me in it?"

"This afternoon, from my window. Saw you pull up, then walk across the campus. What kind of car is it?"

An unbelieving expression crossed Harry's round face. "It's a Porsche! You couldn't tell?" he said with surprise.

"It's beautiful. How fast will it go?"

"Plenty fast, believe me." Harry glanced away at a group which was leaving, then turned to Ben. "Is your dad retired, Ben?"

"Why do you ask?"

"You said you're from Tesuque, just curious. A lot of retired people there."

"No, I don't have a father," Ben replied cautiously. "He left us when I was thirteen."

"Sorry to hear that. So your parents are divorced?"

Ben looked away then dropped his stare to the napkin on the table. "Not really. Listen, Harry, I've got to go. Need to study."

"What business is he in?"

"Farming," said Ben evenly.

"Really?" Got a lot of land up there in Tesuque?"

"Not much. We sold our chilies in town off a card table." Ben noticed Harry's perplexed expression and began to collect his books.

"Don't go Ben. Let me ask you, what kind of name is Touchstone? American?"

Ben fell quiet as he leaned back against the booth then cut his eyes to Harry who quickly looked away. Ben spoke in a hard, modulated voice. "The name Touchstone is a thousand years old. Say it with respect." His solemn expression locked on Harry's face. "My father's a full-blood Tesuque Indian. I'm half white, my mother's an Anglo. I don't give a damn what you or anybody else here thinks. I got a mother back home who's sick and a younger brother that's an alcoholic like my father. I'm here to get an education, so I can get a descent job to help them out. Now you got the picture, Harry?"

Harry studied his empty plate, angry with himself for his impulsive remarks. Strangely, upsetting Ben seemed the last thing he intended. He avoided eye contact and several moments passed in silence. Then Ben stood to leave.

"Ben, I'm sorry. I really am. I didn't know," emoted Harry in his finest portrayal of contrition.

Ben turned and saw Harry staring back with his large brown eyes which seemed sincere. "I mean it, Ben. I think you're a good guy. I like your honesty. Maybe I can help you out, show you a few things. Introduce you to other people. I'd like to, if you'd let me."

For several moments Ben considered what Harry had said. "O.K., Harry. You didn't know. I shouldn't have gotten so tense. It's just that. . . ."

"Tell you what Ben. Someday next week, we'll take the Porsche out, and you can drive it. Sound O.K.?"

"I'd like that," replied Ben as he turned and made his way past empty tables and booths, then slowly crossed the yard toward his room.

At nine the next morning, the executive assistant in Dallas put the call on hold. The light blinked for several seconds, then John Northcutt's voice crackled through the receiver. "Harry, what is it? I'm busy."

"How's mom?"

"Margaret's fine. What d'ya need, son? I'm flying to Houston in half an hour."

"You won't believe who I met last night in the cafeteria?"

"Get on with it, I'm in a hurry."

"An Indian boy who works for the Sneeds here in Santa Fe. Practically lives with them. He could be a gold mine of personal information." John quickly pressed the button instructing his assistant he was not to be interrupted. "Has he been with them long?" John asked.

"Worked there all summer. In and out of the house all day long, including Sneed's office at home. Ben works on weekends now."

Except for John's elevated breathing, Harry heard nothing for several seconds, then John lit a cigarette and cleared his throat. "Did the kid talk about Sneed or his new wife? I heard he's married a little blonde honey from Houston, a socialite wannabe, who's young enough to be his daughter. Did he say anything about her?"

"No, not yet, but I set the hook. I promised him he could drive the Porsche. Just give me time."

"Do whatever it takes, Harry, but be subtle. Don't let him know what you're doing, you'll loose him for sure. Sneed will pay for what he did. I'm proud of you son, you know how much this means to me. I've got to catch a plane. Goodbye."

During the following week, Ben drove the Porsche twice. The more Ben was around Harry, the more he liked him. Harry treated him as an equal, unlike others who tended to ignore him. Harry knew his family background, but he'd accepted him the way he was. Harry had promised Ben he'd never tell a soul about it. Ben believed him. For the first time while at school, Ben felt he'd found a friend, although a strange one.

Ben's circle of friends widened. Harry continued to include him as autumn moved into winter. Ben's grades were good, considering the classes he was taking, and the letters from Kate showed how pleased she was that he was doing well. Ben read each letter twice and kept them neatly folded in the corner of his dresser.

His life was changing and he was thrilled. He finally knew how it felt to be accepted, not just by anyone, but by Harry Northcutt, probably the richest and most popular student at Saint John's. Life was beginning to agree with him.

ELEVEN

On December tenth, Ben woke to the first snow of winter. It had come in the night, quietly, like leaves floating on a river. He reached for the letter from Kate and read it once more. Henry wasn't causing trouble and she planned for them to attend Christmas Mass together in the church at the pueblo. He sensed stress in the way she worded the letter, which caused him worry.

He rolled from bed, dressed, gathered his books and walked across the courtyard. The sidewalks had disappeared, hidden under the snow which was now piled beside the entrance to the cafeteria. He sat sipping coffee and glanced occasionally at the overdue book on English literature. Then suddenly, the idea came to him, as sudden as the snowfall. He would ask Harry to join them for Christmas supper in Tesuque.

Kate readied the table with the biscochitos and bread she'd fried the day before. She was grateful for the weather. It was cold but clear, safe weather for Ben to travel with his friend. She recalled the heavy snow on Christmas the year before as she lowered the burner and stirred the green chili stew bubbling in the iron pot beside her elbow.

At that same moment, Ben's eyes were sweeping the leather dashboard. He turned to stare at the boxes in the back, wrapped in silver paper which shimmered in the brilliant light. He glanced sideways at Harry, his hands locked on the wheel as they darted in and out of the traffic which was moving north to Taos.

"I've never been to an Indian pueblo," said Harry as he accelerated and gently turned the wheel to pass a cattle truck.

"I don't live in the pueblo, Harry, but just across the river from it. Want to see it?"

"Absolutely. Always wanted to see one. Never had the chance 'till I met you."

"No problem."

"Will Henry be there?"

"He should be. Kate would kill him if he didn't show for Christmas supper."

Harry shifted gears as they climbed higher out of Santa Fe. "Here's the road where the Sneeds live," said Ben with pride. Harry slowed and saw the small green sign, Circle Drive, whip past the window. "Heard Mr. Sneed has a new wife? What's she like?"

"Good looking woman. She's half his age," said Ben as he pushed further back into the smooth leather seat.

"They have a lot of parties?"

"A few. I stayed for one of them. Cleaned up the kitchen and kept buckets filled with ice."

"They go on pretty late?" asked Harry as he glanced in the mirror at the car closing on his bumper.

"That one did. It was two in the morning before their friends left. Lots of drinking, I can tell you that."

"Really?"

"Yeah. Mr. Sneed can put away the booze. You need to be in the left lane, Harry. We're almost at the Billco Carpet sign." Harry switched lanes and six miles later turned off the highway onto the hard, dirt road.

"Your mother knows I'm coming?"

"Sure. She wants to meet you. Harry, I said my place is nothing fancy. Just an old adobe house across the river from the pueblo."

"Looking forward to it Ben. I'm flattered you invited me." Ben smiled.

The wire fence was level with the juniper bushes as Harry slowed the Porsche on the narrow road, then saw the meager home and the porch which listed at an angle. The weeds around the house needed cutting, he thought. Harry saw the tattered screens and cardboard squares filling holes in broken windows and the brown, rust stained roof.

Kate turned at the sound of tires in the driveway. She closed the oven, tossed her apron on the counter and watched as Ben and Harry moved toward the porch.

113

"You're finally home!" Kate shouted as she hugged Ben, then turned toward Harry. "Mother, this is Harry Northcutt, my friend at school."

Harry offered his soft hand then said warmly, "It's so good to meet you. Ben says the nicest things about you, Mrs. Touchstone. It's very thoughtful of you to have me."

Kate smiled at Harry and led the way into the kitchen. Ben returned with the gifts, which he placed on the floor beside the tree, adorned with Kate's traditional foil ornaments reflecting the single strand of lights. Ben inhaled the pungent smell of cedar and his mind wandered back to Cundiyo canyon and the fishing trip with Luther, then pictured Two Crows' wrinkled face as he touched the silver chain around his neck.

"I'd like you to meet Henry, Ben's brother," said Kate as she motioned to Henry who was sitting at the table.

"Nice to meet you Henry," said Harry as he cut his eyes around the small room to observe the heater glowing in the corner and the worn sofa by the window. Henry looked past Harry at the boxes by the tree. "Is one of those for me?"

"Of course, Henry," said Harry in a big voice. "You want to open your's first?"

"We'd better wait," said Kate in a nervous tone. "Ben, help me serve the food." Ben watched Kate move slowly to the stove, then falter while she ladled posole into large, clay bowls. He sensed something was wrong. Ben glanced at Henry whose brooding eyes were fixed on the largest silver box beneath the tree.

They ate in silence, except for Harry, who held forth on the long-term benefits of a liberal education. After Kate had cleared the table, Henry continued to stare at the box he thought for certain was his. Harry wiped his mouth with a paper napkin, then with a sweeping gesture of his arm, asked, "Should we open presents?"

Minutes later Kate admired the silk scarf she arranged around her neck. Ben smiled and clutched the shirts and sweater Harry had purchased on the plaza. Henry opened the smallest of the boxes, containing a cap and knitted gloves which he shoved into his jeans. Harry excused himself and made his way to the only bathroom in the house and without speaking, Henry opened the door, crossed the porch and walked slowly down the road toward the bridge.

"Thank you, Mrs. Touchstone for a wonderful meal. I really must go. Ben, thanks for everything, I'll see you back at school. Merry Christmas."

Ben watched Harry back slowly from the drive, then wave as the car picked up speed. When the bell clanged for Mass, Ben glanced out the window at the bridge. Henry was nowhere to be found. He took Kate's arm and led her down the drive toward the river, moving at a slow pace, as if a heavy thing lay across their shoulders.

The church was almost full. A piñon branch rested by the creche with its small painted statues carved from wood. Kate stared at the figure of Mary. Ben studied the animals, their heads bowed before the Child. Kate prayed for Henry, her eyes locked on the lifelike crucifix hanging limp above the altar, staring back at her with large, sad eyes.

From her bedroom window at the pueblo, Pilar Ocate had an unrestricted view of the small adobe house. Earlier in the day, she'd watched the sports car turn into the drive.

She stretched her arms and pressed the pillow against her bare stomach, which was the color of chocolate coated candy, then ran a brush through her long, black hair. She added makeup and studied her slender hips and legs which she flexed in the mirror before pulling on the jeans.

Pilar was determined to have Ben Touchstone before he left for school.

From the window, Pilar watched Kate take her place beside Amelia in the Chevrolet. Father Ortiz, seated in back, waved to Ben who was standing on the porch. Amelia had said she felt honored to drive Father Ortiz to the rectory in Chimayo, and that she and Kate would stay for Christmas Mass which he would offer later in the day.

Minutes later, Ben heard footsteps on the porch and made his way from the kitchen sink toward the door. Probably Henry, he thought.

"Ben, it's Pilar. Open up, I'm cold."

Ben stared down into the large, olive colored eyes. The sweater, barely buttoned, exposed the tops of her high, round breasts. She glided past him, turned, then fixed him in her eyes. "You look good Ben, how's school?"

Ben's surprised gaze then took in her full, red lips which she moistened with her tongue. He swallowed and answered, "O.K. You look good too. Your mother just picked up Kate. They're taking Father Ortiz back to Chimayo."

"I know, she told me," said Pilar in a low, velvet voice as she moved slowly across the floor and locked the door. Ben watched her pull the curtain and smile as she drew up close to him, only inches from his face. "I've missed you Ben. I felt we had a thing going before you left. I've thought about you, all alone in Santa Fe."

Suddenly, Ben felt her long, cold nails behind his neck pull him closer. His breath quickened. His face flushed as he felt her fingers touch the buckle on his belt.

"Ben. Ben Touchstone?" shouted a deep voice through the kitchen door. Ben jerked back from Pilar, who quickly buttoned her blouse. "Ben, are you here?"

Ben unlocked the door and stared at Nando, holding a small, clay pot between his thick, stubby fingers.

"Nando! What are you doing here? How did you find me?" asked Ben with disbelief.

"The people at the school told me where you lived. I had to bring you something. Look, Ben, it bloomed."

Ben peered down at the green stems and the majestic, red flowers quivering in Nando's hands which were shaking from the cold wind whipping through the porch.

"Tulips?" asked Ben as he continued to stare at the crimson blooms.

"Remember Ben? You planted the bulb under the cottonwoods the day we visited in the greenhouse. It bloomed once that spring, then died. Yesterday, Christmas Eve, I found it blooming! This has never happened! It's yours. You planted it. I wanted you to have it. Merry Christmas, Ben."

Ben blinked, then raised his eyes to Nando who smiled and turned to walk slowly down the drive.

"Don't go Nando, I want to talk with you."

Nando never looked back, but waved from the road which would take him back to Santa Fe. He left so quietly, it was as if he had never been there.

"Who was that?" asked Pilar who quickly made her way out the door when she saw her mother's car at a distance, kicking up dust on the road.

"A friend of mine. I wish he'd stayed. I miss him," said Ben as Kate slammed the door and waved goodbye to Amelia, who had motioned for Pilar to join her in the car.

"Did you have a nice visit with Pilar?" asked Kate from the doorway.

"Yeah, O.K., but Nando came by. Did you see him walking on the road?"

"Who?"

"Nando, my friend, the groundskeeper at the Indian School. You passed him on the road just now. He brought me this for Christmas."

Kate's mouth opened with surprise and said, "Ben, that's impossible. Tulips bloom only in the spring and no, I didn't see a soul on the road."

Ben blinked and stared at the flowers, then at Kate, who asked, "Where's Henry?"

"Haven't seen him since this morning," answered Ben, while he continued to gaze at the bright, red blooms. "He'll be back tonight for leftovers," he said, then added, "Leon and Luther said they'd take me back to school."

"When, son?"

"Tonight. I've got finals coming up. I need to study," he replied as he watched Kate's eyes shift to the floorboards of the porch. A moment later, she turned and moved slowly down the hall toward her room.

Late that evening in the library, Ben was hunched over books strewn across the table. He pondered what Nando had given him, then thought of Kate who was alone in bed, staring at the statue while rosary beads clicked slowly through her fingers.

TWELVE

It was the end of May and Ben expected to graduate in December. Fifteen more credit hours, he thought, and he would have his degree. To Ben, the semesters seemed to pass quickly, too quickly. Kate's health was now stable and Henry had managed to stay in school at Santa Clara. The year before, Ben had run for student council president and won. He enjoyed the increased popularity and acceptance the office gave him and referred to his campaign efforts as political maneuvers. Even though a year had passed since his election, the process continued to intrigue him.

Life had been good to him, Ben thought, as he studied the flowers massed around the pool and closer to the house, cosmos and zinnias bursting forth like rainbows. Yarrow plants, heavy with large, lemon colored blooms, shuddered from a breeze which brought the fragrance of cologne as Baxter Sneed walked toward him from the far end of the portal.

Dressed in tan gabardine slacks, madras shirt and double breasted blazer, he unfolded the paycheck and handed it to Ben who leaned against the railing.

"The place looks good, Ben."

"I try," replied Ben distantly while staring down the hill at the highway which snaked toward Taos.

"You like Saint John's, don't you?"

"Yes. Quite a bit. I've learned about things I never knew existed."

"Fine school. How's your grades?" asked Baxter while shielding his eyes from the sun which glared across the portal.

"Made the dean's list the last two years."

"Really? I'm impressed."

"Thanks," said Ben before he straightened and moved toward the steps.

"Ever thought of full time work?" asked Baxter in a cautious tone. Ben turned and replied, "Yes, when I graduate."

118

"No, I mean before that."

"I can't get a decent job without a degree. No one would hire me."

"Ever thought of oil and gas?"

"Never crossed my mind," answered Ben.

"I need a landman, someone local, who knows the people on the pueblos north of here. You know my company has an office in Albuquerque?"

"I've heard you mention it."

"Thirty thousand a year to start with, Ben. If you're good at it, forty thousand the next year. That wouldn't be an unreasonable sum of money to expect."

Ben's eyes snapped toward Baxter, who closely studied Ben's reaction.

"Are you telling me, that if I went to work for you full time, that you would pay me thirty thousand dollars a year?"

"Precisely, Ben, maybe more," said Baxter as he shot a glance to Ben across the portal. "Give it some thought. I've got to leave for Dallas. We can talk when I return."

Baxter disappeared through the door which led to the bedroom off the portal. A moment later, Ben heard the engine start, then the metal gate squeaked open as Baxter turned down Circle Drive.

Ben wiped perspiration from his upper lip, shoved the check into his jeans and crossed the portal to the steps leading down to the pool. He paused and glimpsed the top of the wide brimmed hat propped on Morgan's head. From his perspective, two bare feet extended from underneath the brim.

"Ben, is that you up there?"

"Yes, it's me, Mrs. Sneed."

"Did Baxter leave?"

"Yes."

"Bring me a towel from my bedroom, will you? There's one on the stool beside my dresser," she said in a voice loud enough to carry from the pool and up the steps to the portal. Ben walked through the open door, found the white cotton towel, then made his way down toward the oversized hat.

"Thank you Ben," said Morgan in a pleasant tone when she heard his boots on the steps. Then in a low voice, "Come here Ben, I want to show you something." He drew closer, then realized she was completely nude, sprawled across the lounger. One leg was propped up, leaving nothing to his imagination. Ben stared for a moment, then looked away to the deep end of the pool.

"What's wrong, Ben? Haven't you seen a woman's body before? Sunbathing nude is something I enjoy. It's healthy, don't you know?"

"No, I didn't," said Ben quietly as he moved his eyes sideways to glimpse her tanned, lean figure. She pulled off the hat and tossed it on the concrete to expose her streaked blonde hair, woven in a thick braid which draped across her shoulder. "Bring me the towel Ben, put it on the lounger."

Ben moved closer and became aroused as he studied the firm breasts which shifted as Morgan slid further down the lounger. Ben moved within inches of her arm and dropped the towel beside her elbow.

"Like what you see, Ben?"

Ben nodded slowly, but paused for several moments before he looked away. Suddenly, his eyes jerked toward the side entrance leading to the pool. Behind the gate, something moved. Harry Northcutt was smiling through the bars.

Morgan turned and watched Harry run from the gate down the driveway. She grabbed the towel, covered herself, then cut her eyes to Ben.

"Ben? Who the hell was that?" she snapped.

"A friend from school," Ben said awkwardly. "He was coming to pick me up. I forgot," he stammered as Morgan shot bolt upright on the lounger.

"He saw me naked, Ben! What do you intend to do about it? I have a reputation to uphold," shouted Morgan in a hard voice as she knotted the towel under her arm, then walked quickly up the stairs toward her bedroom.

Ben stared at the empty driveway, then to Morgan rushing down the portal. She slammed and locked the bedroom door.

Ben sensed something bad was about to happen, but it would be some time later before he found how really bad it was to be.

THIRTEEN

B less me father for I have sinned," Ben murmured through the grating of the confessional, tucked in the corner of the church which overlooked the pueblo.

"Hello, Ben, I recognized your voice. Is anything wrong?" asked Father Ortiz who pulled at the stiff plastic collar, a notch of white at the center of his throat.

"I need to talk," replied Ben in the closeness of the hot, cramped stall.

"I'm listening," said the elderly priest, who wiped sweat from his wrinkled forehead.

"Remember the Christmas when mother and Amelia Ocate drove you back to Chimayo after Mass here in Tesuque?"

"Yes?"

"A girl came to see me," said Ben, who now lowered his voice to a whisper.

"And?"

"She wanted to make love. I didn't try to stop her, but someone knocked on the door. She left right after that."

"What else, Ben?" said Father Ortiz, his faded eyes resting on the rosary which moved slowly through his thin, bent fingers.

"Last week, while I was working at the house on Circle Drive, the owner's wife, who was lying by the pool, asked me to bring her a towel. When I got closer, I saw. . . ."

"Finish, Ben."

"She was naked. Then she asked me to come closer."

"Did you?"

"Yes, and I stared at her for a long time. I got aroused. Then I saw someone staring from the gate beside the driveway," said Ben, who dropped his eyes to his hands which were folded on his chest.

121

"Anything else?" asked the priest, who drew in shallow breaths within the confines of the box.

"Just before that happened, her husband offered me a job."

"I thought you worked for him already?"

"I mean a real job, working for his oil company. He offered me thirty thousand dollars a year. The second year, he said, I could make forty thousand. I don't know what to do, father."

"Are your grades good at college?"

"Yes, I'm on the dean's list."

"And you've only got one more semester before you graduate?"

"That's right," answered Ben who moved his eyes up to stare through the grating at the lace cloth separating him from Father Ortiz.

"Will you lose your scholarship if you go to work for this man?"

"No, I spoke to my counselor at school. She said they'd let me return and finish my classes if the job didn't work out."

"What does Kate think?"

"Haven't spoken to her yet."

"If you continue at school, you'll still be working at their house and the wife will be there everyday?" asked the priest in a guarded tone.

"Yes, for the rest of this summer. Next fall I'll work on weekends."

The old man fell silent. Ben heard the beads clicking on his fingernails. A minute passed before the priest said, "Ben if I were you. . . ." He paused again, cleared his throat and continued, "If I were you, I'd take the job. That's a lot of money, Ben."

"I know."

"If things don't work out, you can always return to school. Besides, Kate could use some comforts for a change."

"I've thought of that," said Ben while shifting his weight on the hard, wooden kneeler.

"But more importantly, if you continue working at their home, this woman will be a constant occasion of sin for you. Grave sin."

Ben's eyes darted from the cloth to the small brass crucifix above the grating, then murmured, "I know. Thank you father, for your advice."

"Anytime, Ben. Now go in peace, and give my love to Kate."

Two days later, Ben stood beside the Porsche parked in the shadow of the dormitory. The trunk was open and Ben stared at the smooth leather bags, the initials, H.N. stamped below the handles. A tennis racket and fishing reel were shoved into a corner.

Ben dreaded meeting Harry who was turning the corner, his arms filled with shirts and sweaters piled above thick, round shoulders.

"Hello, Harry," Ben said, as Harry dropped the clothes into the trunk. "Going back to Dallas?"

"Yeah. But only for a few days. Want to visit my friends. My parents have rented me an apartment here in Santa Fe. Dallas is hot as hell in the summer. How you been?"

"O.K., I suppose. Harry, it's about the other day," he said cautiously.

"You mean by the Sneed's pool?"

"Yeah. Nothing happened, Harry. When Mrs. Sneed saw you, she wrapped herself in the towel and disappeared into the house."

"Sure, Ben. I can guess what happened, you don't need to elaborate."

Ben looked away, shrugged, then said, "Harry, I've been offered a full time job by Mr. Sneed. I'm going to be working as a landman for his oil company."

Harry paused for several moments while staring at the tennis racket, then asked, "You're dropping out of school? You've only got one more semester."

"They're giving me the time off. If things don't work out with Sneed Oil, then I can return."

"Sounds like a great deal, Ben. I suppose Sneed is paying you well?"

"Thirty thousand the first year, maybe more the next."

Harry rolled his large eyes to demonstrate to Ben he was suitably impressed. "How did he come to hire you?"

"Said he needed a local to work some leases. Someone who knew the people north of here, who live in the pueblos."

"Sneed plans to do some drilling up there?" asked Harry, whose mind was moving faster than Ben could answer.

"I guess."

"When do you start?"

"Soon. But there's a lengthy training session for new employees. I need to buy some clothes, and find a place to live in Albuquerque. He even offered me a company car."

Harry continued processing the bits of data which raced through his mind, then said, "I'm happy for you, Ben. Look, I've got to go, got a twelve hour drive to Dallas. I'll be back soon. Let's get together."

Ben watched the Porsche pull from the parking lot, twist down the hill, then point south toward the interstate. Harry punched the keypad on the phone beside his elbow. "Hello, Barbara, it's Harry, put me through to father. I'm in my car, heading for Dallas. Tell him it's important."

FOURTEEN

Ben sipped coffee on the small balcony of the apartment which surveyed the shopping center parking lot four miles from the center of Albuquerque. That morning while dressing, he discovered the silver cross and chain had disappeared. He had frantically searched the apartment. He looked behind drapes, underneath the bed, even in the new company car parked beneath the balcony. It had vanished. But why hadn't he noticed until now? He had worked in the flower beds on Circle Drive. Maybe he had lost it there? But that was sometime ago. Stunned by the loss and his lack of observation, he shifted his thoughts to the past weeks of endless seminars, charts and graphs. He stared down past the tan slacks at his loafers, similar to Harry's, he thought, then glanced at the Buick below the balcony. His life had changed and he was grateful. Without Harry's help and friendship, Ben knew he'd have been lost in the modern, Anglo world. Below, people pushed carts from the supermarket to their cars, then abandoned them for someone else to return.

He walked into the living room and thumbed through papers he lifted from the leather briefcase. Baxter had told him it wasn't such an important deal, just something to get him started. To Ben, it was the biggest thing he'd ever undertaken.

The top line, printed in bold type read: OIL AND GAS LEASE. On the following line, in smaller type was: Aspen Ranch, Tesuque. His eyes scanned to the beginning of the first paragraph: *"Sneed Oil Inc., proposes to develop a field of petroleum production, adjacent to, and including, mineral rights held and owned by the people of the Tesuque Nation, herein referred to as, Tesuque Pueblo."* The terms of the lease continued, *"Sneed Oil Inc., seeks to acquire mineral rights on the 318.05 acre tract referred to by the New Mexico Bureau of Land as Aspen Ranch. This parcel, acquired by Tesuque Pueblo in a compensation purchase agreement dated, May 1, 1937, is owned and operated as a wildlife refuge by the Tesuque Pueblo."* The lease concluded: *"A reasonable and fair market purchase price of one hundred dollars per acre is hereby offered to the designated Tesuque Pueblo representative, by Sneed Oil Inc., on or before midnight of the date named above."* It was signed in a large scroll: Baxter Sneed, President, Sneed Oil Inc.

At dawn on Monday, Ben stood quietly at the edge of the mesa and waited. Papers stacked on the hood of the Buick were ruffled by wind which drove down the mountain through a stand of aspens. Within the trees, a hundred yards away, he saw the tall man move toward the clearing. A single eagle feather jutted from his head. In the distance, Ben watched the man move toward him, cautiously, as if he was stalking animals.

Low, gray clouds moved across the mesa as light rain began to spit across the windshield. The man was only fifty feet away when Ben realized it was Luther dressed in boots, denim shirt and jeans. Luther didn't smile. Ben walked toward him and extended his hand. Luther folded his arms and stared out across the valley beneath the mesa, his long, black hair blowing in the wind.

Ben spoke first. "Luther, I didn't know you'd be here. How you been?"

"Ben, you are my oldest friend, " said Luther in a low, even voice. "I heard you'd gone to work, but for this company? I just don't understand you."

"What do you mean. . . this company?"

"You don't know?"

"Know what?"

"For years, Sneed Oil has been buying up land all around us. They've cut and cleared a thousand acres of our hunting grounds. When they drill for oil, they build roads, then large trucks drive through the forest, disturbing the animals who have called it home for decades. Even the rivers are polluted from the open tanks they dig beside the wells and fill with chemicals."

Ben fell silent and looked down at his loafers which were covered with

126

then glanced at Luther and said, "It's my job, Luther, I hope you understand."

"I will never understand. Your people have robbed us for many, many years. Now you want to steal what little we have left. No, Ben I will never understand."

Ben was stunned. He looked away from Luther, who continued to stare into the valley.

"You just called me Anglo. I can't believe you said that. I have Tesuque blood running through my veins."

"You may have, Ben, but you look and talk like the Anglos who came before you, the ones Leon ran off. I fear deeply for our people's future, just like Leon does. I've been elected by the pueblo to deal with outsiders."

Ben stared into Luther's dark eyes, set deep into his face, then saw the creases which had formed above his cheekbones. Sorrow swept through Ben's heart and his stomach churned from the things Luther had said. He felt sick as he turned away to leave.

"Wait, Ben. I have something to show you." Luther removed the folded sheet of paper from his jeans and handed it to Ben. Ben looked away to try and hide the tears which filled his eyes. "Read it Ben. This Anglo came to my home late last night. Told me he was a close friend of yours. Said he knew Kate, even had Christmas dinner with your family. I introduced him to Leon and my mother, then asked him in to talk. This is what he left us."

Ben wiped his face then glanced at the creased paper which began, *"Oil and gas lease offered to the Tesuque Pueblo of New Mexico, of one hundred fifty dollars per acre, for all or part of their mineral rights to a 318.05 acre tract, referred to as, Aspen Ranch."* Ben's eyes dropped to the signature at the bottom of the lease: Harry Northcutt, Northcutt Exploration.

"Ben, what's your company's offer?" asked Luther in a distant voice.

Ben's dazed expression shifted from Luther to the papers on the hood.

"I think a hundred an acre was the most we'd pay," Ben replied through the rising wind, whipping rain into pellets which stung his face. "I'm sorry, Luther. I didn't know you'd be the one I'd talk to. Please understand, it's my job," shouted Ben as Luther turned and walked through the driving rain toward the stand of aspens. Ben braced himself against the hood and watched his papers being swept into the air above his head. Tears streamed down his face and mingled with the rain as Ben watched Luther disappear into the trees.

The next morning at his office in Albuquerque, Ben cradled the receiver and waited for the operator to find the listing in Santa Fe. He dialed the number.

"Hello," answered the nasal voice.

"Harry, it's Ben Touchstone. I was up at Aspen Ranch yesterday. Heard you paid Luther Moquino a visit the night before. What's going on, Harry, I thought you were my friend?"

"Oh, that? It's nothing, Ben. Just doing a little business for my dad. He handed me the lease while I was walking out the door. Is Sneed Oil interested in leasing it?"

"Yes, we are. It's my deal, my very first deal, Harry."

Harry reached for a cigarette, struck a match and blew smoke across the bedroom of his apartment. "Did you make the guy an offer?"

"Yes, but forget it Harry, the Tesuque tribal council won't ever lease that land. Trust me, I know what I'm talking about."

"How is Mrs. Sneed?" asked Harry as he reached for the cold cup of coffee he'd brewed the day before.

"How would I know?" Why do you ask such a thing?"

"Well. . . after I saw you and her by the pool. . . ."

"Harry, I told you once, nothing happened, understand?" said Ben tersely.

"You should see the blowups," said Harry as he sipped the coffee.

"You took pictures?"

"Sure, including you, standing by the lounger, gawking."

"I don't believe you."

"Believe me, Ben. I've got several here I'm looking at right now. Want me to tell you the color of her. . . ."

"That's enough. You show those to anyone and I'll. . . ."

"You'll do what Ben? Sue me? After all, you asked me to pick you up. I just happened to be there when. . . ."

"I want the negatives, Harry, I mean it. I want them today."

"That's a possibility!" snapped Harry. "I say we meet for lunch, talk this over like gentlemen."

"Where, what time?" asked Ben anxiously.

"Pranzo, next to Sanbusco Center here in Santa Fe. Meet me there this afternoon, at one."

Two hours later, Ben was ushered to the booth in the corner of the crowded restaurant. He glanced across the linen cloth at Harry who pinched an empty highball glass between his short, wide fingers. His other hand offered Ben a piece of bread, smeared with garlic and tomatoes. Ben waited as Harry motioned to the waiter to bring another drink. Harry asked quietly, "Any other wildcat wells I should know about?"

"What wells?" asked Ben in a puzzled tone.

"At Sneed Oil, of course."

"Why should I tell you?"

"Let's say you owe me, Ben," said Harry while staring over the rim of the gin and tonic.

Ben shook his head in disbelief.

"Think about it, Ben. I introduced you to all your friends at school, taught you how to dress, how to handle yourself around other people."

"I appreciate everything, Harry. But sharing inside information about pending developments with someone else. . . I won't do it, Harry, it's wrong. The people at Sneed Oil have put their trust in me."

Harry stirred the drink with his finger, then waited while the waiter placed menus on the table. "We'll order in awhile," said Harry to the waiter who turned and left.

"I heard there's an oil play near the Colorado border, something big. Rumor has it, Sneed leased several hundred acres and drilled a test well. And word has it that he's looking at results from a wildcat well near Hatch? Any truth to any of this?"

"Do I have to repeat myself, Harry? It's wrong what you're asking me to do and you know it," said Ben as his hands gripped the table.

"I'm not asking, Ben, I'm telling. I want all the well information on these wildcats—the samples, mud logs and electrical logs brought to me by noon tomorrow. If not, I'll have to send Baxter Sneed a little something in the mail." Harry slowly reached into the pocket of his blazer and dropped the color photograph in the middle of the table. Ben leaned and saw himself standing over Morgan Sneed.

Ben's face grew pallid. His mouth became dry, then he said in a tense voice, "You wouldn't."

"Try me, Ben. Here's my address. Don't need to call, just be there tomorrow at noon. I'll be waiting." Harry stood, collected the photograph and smiled at Ben before walking quickly through the crowded restaurant.

Ben sat in silence for several minutes. He was confused and alone, more alone than at any other time in his life. Luther had rejected him. Now Harry had asked him to do something very wrong, and if he didn't, Ben was certain of the consequences. He thought of Kate and how the loss of his job would devastate her. "Was this what life was all about?" he wondered to himself as he felt a deep sadness engulf him.

At that moment, the image of his angel snapped into his consciousness. The exact words she'd spoken in the chapel at Chimayo suddenly filled his mind as if she were present in the booth: "Ben, you'll meet many people in your life. Some will be kind and thoughtful but others will be dark, very dark, their souls filled with evil. You won't know the difference between them Ben, but they'll be there and so will I."

The waiter stared at Ben seated alone in the booth. Ben's eyes were fixed on something the waiter couldn't see. He blinked and smiled as if someone had spoken to him, stood, placed a bill on the table and crossed the room toward the entrance.

Moments later, as he cleared the table, the waiter suddenly felt a warmth surround him, then paused at the scent of roses which lingered in the air.

Harry was waiting by the door of the apartment. He offered Ben a beer, which he refused, then they sat on a long, stuffed sofa in the living room.

"Do you really plan to send that picture to Baxter Sneed?" Ben asked.

"To be honest, Ben, I really don't want to. If you hand over the well logs and samples, I'll destroy the negatives."

"I've given it some thought," said Ben before he glanced around the room filled with paintings and antiques. "I really don't care what you do with that photograph. I know what really happened. If you want to send it, go right ahead."

Harry paused a long time before replying, "If that's how you feel, my father is willing to pay you fifty thousand dollars, cash, to provide us with the information on those wells. No questions asked."

Ben hesitated then said, "Fifty thousand dollars? You're joking?"

"No I'm not."

Ben thought of the things he could do with such a large sum of money, including an addition to the house in Tesuque. He dropped his stare to the carpet and struggled with the offer.

"Take your time, Ben, think it over. Give me a call when you're ready with your answer. You could buy a lot of things with fifty thousand dollars."

"I know," Ben sighed as he stood and walked slowly through the door. A week passed. He had waited long enough. Harry Northcutt sat quietly in the Porsche at the bottom of the hill. Smoke drifted from his nostrils, his eyes riveted on the gate which protected the large adobe house on Circle Drive. Ten minutes later the gate opened and Harry watched the Lincoln pull slowly from the drive. As it neared, Harry turned away, then waited until the dust settled before he walked to the gate and pressed the button above the mailbox.

From the speaker, partly hidden by a piñon tree, came a woman's voice, "Yes, who is it?"

"U.P.S., ma'am."

"Leave it in the mailbox, I'll get it in a minute."

Harry gently dropped the small, unmarked envelope into the box and moved quickly along the adobe wall toward the Porsche.

Minutes later in the kitchen, Morgan Sneed slit the envelope, then gasped at the photographs which fell to the floor. She knelt and quietly read the typed note which lay beside the pictures;

"Dear Mrs. Sneed,

Enclosed are some pictures I thought you'd be interested in seeing. I know Baxter would be thrilled to see them, or anybody else in Santa Fe, Dallas, or maybe even Houston. To receive the negatives, simply ask Ben Touchstone to deliver the package. He'll know what to bring. Have him drop it at the main gate of the cemetery across from De Vargas mall at eight o'clock tonight. Have him come alone, drop the package and drive away. I'll be watching, Mrs. Sneed. Make sure he comes alone. I've truly enjoyed meeting you in such a personal way. An admirer."

Morgan rushed to the telephone hanging on the wall beside the bar. "Information, I need the number for Ben Touchstone in Albuquerque," she snapped while her tangerine nails rapped against the counter. She stared across the property at the flowers Ben had grown from seed then quickly dialed the number.

"Ben?"

"Yes?"

"It's Morgan Sneed. Something terrible has happened."

"To Mr. Sneed?"

"No. Someone just left a package in my mailbox. There are dreadful pictures of us Ben—when I sunbathed by the pool. You're standing next to me. They're appalling."

"Is there a note?"

"Yes. It says for you to deliver some things—it says you'd know—to the main gate of the cemetery across from De Vargas mall at eight o'clock tonight. What's this all about, Ben? It's the worst thing that's ever happened to me!" sobbed Morgan through the receiver.

"That son of a bitch," whispered Ben.

"What? Who is it Ben? I have to know."

"Let me handle this. Is Mr. Sneed there now?"

"No, thank God. He drove off just before. . . ."

"Tear them up and burn them."

"Then what?"

"I'll drop the package at the cemetery tonight. You'll never hear from him again. Trust me Mrs. Sneed, you can count on it."

Ben replaced the receiver and stared out into space. His face took on a strange tenseness as he reached for the keys. It would be a day Ben would regret for the rest of his life.

Twenty four hours later, Harry Northcutt quickly shifted gears in the Porsche, moving north toward the Colorado border at ninety miles per hour. Sinclair Reed, another landman for Northcutt Exploration was on another interstate, speeding south toward the small town of Hatch, just sixty miles from Texas. They both hoped Baxter Sneed had given the landowners thirty day drafts to lease their land. If so, they would offer even more per acre and secure signed leases with cashier's checks made payable to the owners that afternoon. It was undoubtedly worth the effort; the electric logs and samples had shown there were vast amounts of crude below the surface of both leases, plus the samples near Hatch confirmed natural gas reserves to be the biggest find in years. By sundown both held signed leases in their hands.

FIFTEEN

Three years later, in the tenth floor suite above the Albuquerque freeway, Ben nodded to his secretary who handed him the note. He studied her long, lean legs as she moved gracefully across the beige colored carpet. Baxter Sneed had appointed him Director of Media Relations, which was etched into a slab of crystal resting on his desk. The secretary came with the new title.

His eyes quickly scanned the note from Haley Hoffman confirming their tennis match and dinner at the country club later that evening. Settling deeper into the high-backed chair, Ben stared through the broad window at snow clinging to Sandia peak, then jotted down the number the operator had given him and waited for the dial tone. The phone in Tesuque rang four times, then he heard the fragile voice through the handset. "Ben, is that you?"

"Hello, mother. How do you like your new phone? I am speaking up. Can you hear me now?" asked Ben as he smiled at the secretary, who had returned with a memo which she placed beside the telephone.

"How is Henry?"

"He's moved out, Ben. He's living with Pilar Ocate in an apartment in Española. Amelia is sick about it. So am I. Neither one of them have jobs and Amelia heard his drinking's gotten worse. I'm at my wits end with Henry."

"You said he'd gotten a job in Santa Cruz."

"He was fired last week. It's the third time this year. He's becoming like your father after he started drinking."

Ben stared somberly through the window and pictured Ojo's face in the photograph which Kate kept beside her bed, then said, "Mother, you've got to realize that Henry's grown. He's almost twenty-two. Stop worrying about him. There's nothing you can do."

"I can pray, like I pray for you," said Kate, her voice gaining strength. "How was your visit to the doctor?"

"All right, I suppose. He said my heart's a little weaker but it's still ticking."

"How is Amelia?"

"She's fine. She drove me to the doctor." Kate drew in a deep breath before saying with concern, "There's something important I want tell you."

"What is it?"

"It's about Luther."

"What about him?"

"He's called me every other day. He's even come to visit at least four or five times during the last two weeks."

"Why?" asked Ben.

"He feels bad about what happened between you two on the mesa— when you met about that oil lease. He told me all about it. You and Luther are the oldest of friends. Something like that should never come between you. Like I said, he feels badly about the way he treated you. He wants to know if you'll even speak to him again. He wanted your home number in Albuquerque, so I gave it to him. Was that all right?"

"Of course. Tell Luther I'd like to see him. We have some talking to do."

"You know he's been elected to Lieutenant Governor of the pueblo?"

"No, I didn't know. That pleases me. Ask him to call anytime. Has your new bed been delivered? Are you sleeping better?"

"Yes, it was nice what you did."

"Is Father Ortiz out of the hospital?"

"No, they say he has to stay there for awhile. Needs the rest after his heart attack."

"I'm glad he's doing well. I've got good news."

"What son?"

"I've been promoted to assistant vice president," said Ben with pride.

"How wonderful!" exclaimed Kate, then whispered, "did you get a raise?"

"Yes, mother, I got a raise. What do you think helped pay for your new bed?"

"Ben, are you going to Mass, like you said you would?"

"Yes, mother, every Sunday at Sacred Heart Church when I'm in Albuquerque. You know I travel quite a bit, remember?"

"Yes, I know, but there are Catholic churches everywhere you go. Always keep your faith, dear, it's the only thing that's left, after all is said and done," she added gently.

"I will, mother. I have to go. There are two people I need to see. Take good care of yourself and if there's anything you need, just pick up your new telephone. That's what it's for. I love you," said Ben as he replaced the receiver and stood as the tall, broad shouldered man dressed in a navy blue suit, entered, shook hands then sat in a chair beside the desk.

"Mr. Touchstone," the man began in a muted voice. "I represent someone who, for the sake of discretion, shall remain anonymous during our conversation." Ben stood and closed the door and returned to the high-backed chair behind the desk, then leaned forward on his elbows as the man continued. "I have in my briefcase fifty thousand dollars in cash." Ben glanced at the black leather case which the man lifted from the floor and placed in the center of the desk. Two brass latches snapped open and Ben stared down at rows of crisp, hundred dollar bills. Ben continued to stare as the man cleared his throat, "If you accept this, the party I represent will consider his debt from several years past, paid in full."

Ben's eyes shifted from the money to the man across the desk, then returned to the briefcase. He stroked his chin, then said, "I know who you mean. I thought all that had been forgotten. Why is he doing this?"

"I cannot speak for my client, other than what I've said. He did say, though. . . ." The man paused as he crossed his long legs, then continued ". . . that this would be a one time offer. Take it or leave it, Mr Touchstone."

Ben let out a long sigh and closed his eyes. The image of an addition to the house for Kate swept through his mind. He waited for several seconds, then stood and closed the briefcase. The man studied Ben's face: the close cropped blonde hair parted on the side, the small wrinkles at the corners of the cobalt eyes and furrows etched into his forehead. Ben gazed at the briefcase for several moments. With a suddenness, he reached and placed it on the floor behind the desk.

"If I accept it, I want the negatives," Ben said while staring at the case. Without speaking, the man reached into the inside pocket of his jacket and dropped the sealed envelope on the desk. Ben quickly scanned the negatives. "I'll take it," Ben said abruptly.

"It was a pleasure doing business with you, Mr. Touchstone." The man stood and turned to leave, then paused to add, "My client will be very pleased at your decision. Goodbye, Mr. Touchstone."

The man smiled and closed the door behind him, then switched off the small tape recorder in the inside pocket of his jacket.

Several moments later, Baxter Sneed appeared. "Who was that? Never seen him before."

"Said he wants a job in our public relations department. I sent him down to human resources."

"Are you all right, Ben? You look pale."

"I'm fine, just a little tired. You want to meet here, or in your office?"

"Here's fine. I'm on my way to the airport to meet our pilot and fly to Midland. We've bought up a couple of sections in Andrews County. George Lentz, the geologist in our Midland office, believes there might be commercial production from some of those well bores if we recomplete higher up in the Devonian. I bought them for next to nothing."

"How deep were they initially drilled?"

"Down to the Ellenburger."

"That's deep."

"Believe it, Ben. Around thirteen thousand feet. They were all dry holes, except for one well that's making a lot more water than oil. That's why I got them for a song," said Baxter as he studied the lines creasing Ben's forehead and the small pouches beneath his weary eyes. Then Baxter added quickly, "I want you to leave first thing in the morning for Roswell to put out a brush fire. A local T.V. station has been running a series of stories about how the oil industry is ruining New Mexico's environment. Those S.O.B.'s have singled out Sneed Oil. It's all a bunch of rubbish. Sam Gibbons in Exploration will brief you before you go. He's prepared facts and figures which will balance the bullshit they are shoveling out to their viewers across the state. Ben, straighten them out and put a lid on this before it turns into something nasty. I'll be in our Midland office for a couple of days. Call me if you run into problems. Good luck."

At ten that night, Ben sat slumped behind the desk, his haggard face cradled in his hands. Earlier, he had canceled the tennis match and dinner with Haley and spent the remainder of the day conducting two television interviews, announcing Sneed Oil would soon be expanding exploration in the southern half of Arizona. He was exhausted. He studied his reflection in the window and began to dread the trip to Roswell in the morning. The media would be in full attendance as soon as he arrived at the press conference scheduled for two o'clock that afternoon.

The white dress shirt was rolled up past his elbows, the knitted silk tie hung loose around his neck. He stared back at his vacant eyes. He sensed something gnawing at his soul. An unseen force warned him it was time to make a change. He felt hollow inside, empty, like a dry creek before a storm. Then he lifted the receiver and slowly dialed the number.

"Mother, it's Ben."

"It's awfully late, is something wrong?"

"No, I'm fine. Remember, I told you I'd gotten a raise?"

"Yes, son, but you sound troubled."

"No, just tired." Ben paused and glanced down at the briefcase, "I'd like to add onto your house and buy you some new appliances."

"Ben, can you afford it?" Kate asked in a whisper.

"Yes, don't worry. I'll make some calls tomorrow to get things moving. I love you," Ben said before replacing the handset to stare past his reflection at the mangled cars on the freeway, twisted from an accident. He watched lights flashing on an ambulance which parted traffic as it raced toward the victims. He heard sirens wailing and horns, then wished for a moment he was living at Tesuque, in the small adobe house beside the river.

The following week, alone in his truck parked under the shadow of the tall glass building, Luther watched Ben, dressed in business suit and tie, make his way between the rows of cars reserved for visitors. Ben had suggested they meet in his office. Luther wanted them to meet inside his pickup.

"Hello Luther," said Ben as he swung himself into the seat and glanced at two red-tailed hawk feathers suspended from the mirror. From the dashboard, a country western song floated from the speakers.

"Hello Ben," said Luther in a guarded tone as he turned down the volume and offered Ben a coke from the plastic box between the seats.

"I called Kate. I've been to see her several times."

"I know, she told me."

"Didn't know if you'd speak to me after the way I treated you on the mesa that morning."

"Those were pretty strong words, Luther. I felt their effect for a long time."

"I'd like to apologize for judging you so harshly. You were just doing your job."

"Accepted. Now tell me, how are things at Tesuque?"

"The same. Things never change up there. We voted not to lease the land at Aspen Ranch."

"I felt you wouldn't. Don't really blame you. That land is special."

"I was up there the other day and saw an eagle's nest. First one I've seen in years. And the streams are running cold and clear. You been fishing lately?"

Ben let out a long sigh and glanced up at the window of his office and said, "No, not in a long time. I miss our fishing trips, Luther. This job's got me tied down. You been fishing lately?"

"Yeah, almost every week. Caught a German brown on the Pecos the other day, just above Brush Ranch, near Cowles."

"A big one?" asked Ben.

"Went eighteen inches. Almost as big as the rainbow you caught when we camped up in Cundiyo canyon. Remember the trip, Ben? We were still kids."

"Yeah, I think of it often. A lot of incredible things happened on that trip."

"What you did that day—I'll never forget it," said Luther while glancing sideways at Ben.

"What do you mean?"

"When you released that rainbow. You knew it was a trophy fish, but you gave it back its life. I've never admired you more, Ben, watching you hold it in the current until its strength returned, then seeing it move safely into deeper water with its freedom."

Both men stared in silence through the dust covered windshield at the traffic buzzing past them on the freeway. They sat quietly for some time, knowing each other's thoughts as well as their own. Then Ben said, "Luther, I'm really glad you called. I'm sorry also for what happened that morning on the mesa. Your friendship means a lot to me. You're the best and oldest friend I have. You've made a difference in my life. You've given me insight into things that I never would have known, if not for you."

"Thanks for saying that. You know I feel the same. You sound whipped. Something wrong?"

"I'm getting burned out. Seems I barely have time to eat and sleep. One of these days I'd like to lock my office and throw away the key. The income's great, but I'm beginning to realize there's other things more important than money. Know what I mean?"

"For sure. That's where most people screw up. They focus on material possessions and forget about the spiritual side of life."

"Kate said you were elected Lieutenant Governor of the pueblo. That's quite an honor."

"Yeah, it is."

"Is it a political thing?"

"No, not really. I got a call one morning asking if I would serve and I accepted."

"In my junior year at Saint John's, I ran for student council president. Planned my own campaign."

"Did you win?" asked Luther as he lowered the volume of the radio.

"By a landslide. I enjoyed it. . . the challenge, the strategies and meeting new people. My platform called for some serious changes in their system. My ideas were put into effect a month after I was elected. Surprised the hell out of me."

"You ever thought of going into politics?" asked Luther.

"Once, the night the votes were counted in the school cafeteria. But that was a long time ago. Luther, I'm glad you called. Let's get together. . . maybe dinner somewhere in Santa Fe, then we can take in the late show at Vanessie's. By the way, do you ever see Amelia Ocate?"

"Sure. She lives fifty yards from me, just off the plaza. I see her almost every day."

"How's she doing?"

"She's slowing down. She even talks slow."

"Kate thinks a lot of her. She told me she wouldn't know what she'd do without Amelia," said Ben as he glanced out the window at the traffic.

"I've heard Amelia say the very same thing about Kate. They're almost like sisters," added Luther.

"Let's not be strangers, Luther. I'll call you soon."

"You know where to find me."

The two shook hands, then Ben closed the door of the pickup and made his way through the parking lot toward the building. He stood beside the entrance and heard another country western song blaring from the truck. Ben smiled, then saw Luther wave before he blended with the traffic of the freeway.

SIXTEEN

Valet parkers darted between the cars lining Circle Drive. They rushed from the driveway down the hill, almost to the Taos highway, then back, handing out vouchers to the guests who made their way into the large adobe home. An awning had been installed to cover the courtyard in case a sudden shower might disturb the guests who continued to flow through the zaguan into the living room and out onto the portal. They milled around the pool, waiting for the serving line to open, talking, drinking and lifting hors d'oeuvres off trays passed by waiters dressed in black slacks and short, white coats.

A soft breeze ruffled Morgan's thin, silk blouse, as well as her hair, which she'd coiled in braids above her smooth, cultured face. As she sipped the cocktail, Morgan glanced over the rim of the glass at the guests, most of them elegantly dressed, who continued to parade through the tall wooden doors. She greeted several who arrived late, then saw Baxter at the far end of the portal beside the bar, huddled with someone she couldn't recognize.

Conversations floated in and out between the rooms. The women were dressed in what Morgan had referred to on the invitation as Santa Fe Casual, which she knew would range from blue jeans to long silk dresses, which several women wore, and everything in between. It was a glorious party, and Morgan was relishing the response to the invitations she'd sent at Baxter's request, which had been lettered in perfect calligraphy:

> *Mr. & Mrs. Baxter Sneed request the*
> *pleasure of your company for cocktails*
> *and dinner, to celebrate the tenth*
> *anniversary of the opening of Sneed Oil*
> *Company's first office in New Mexico*

Morgan worked her way through their friends and company employees to the end of the portal overlooking the pool. She glanced down at the long row of tables spread with white linen which touched the decking and watched three Hispanic women, dressed in lace aprons and shiny black dresses, ladle shrimp and lobster tails onto plates filled with cream covered pasta. Morgan shifted her gaze to the opposite end of the pool where a large man, wearing a tall chef's hat, sliced medallions from a tenderloin of beef then stuffed them into rolls which he arranged beside the china plates, gleaming under the warm, June sun.

When she turned, she saw Ben standing by the door which led into the kitchen. Dressed in a black jacket, pink knit shirt and tan linen slacks, he was surrounded by a small group of admirers who laughed at almost everything he said. By his side stood a tall thin brunette who wore a beige chiffon pants ensemble which Morgan had seen at Neiman Marcus during her recent buying spree in Dallas. Next Morgan noticed the strands of antique silver beads twined around her long graceful neck. She watched the athletic looking woman lean close to Ben, whisper something in his ear, kiss his cheek then move toward the kitchen. He looked quite handsome she thought, and more mature. Morgan guessed his age at thirty, maybe less, as she lit a cigarette and moved toward him, now alone, standing in the doorway.

"Hello, Ben. It's been quite a while since we've seen each other."

"Yes, it has, Mrs. Sneed."

"Who's your friend?"

"You mean Haley?"

"Is she a local girl?"

"She's from Albuquerque. Met her playing tennis at the club."

"She's quite attractive," said Morgan in a distant tone tinged with jealousy.

"Like you said, it's been awhile. Several years I guess," remarked Ben as he glanced at Haley staring back at him through the kitchen window.

141

"At least," Morgan replied while studying his striking features and the age lines which had formed on his forehead and at the corners of his eyes. "Baxter tells me you've made quite a contribution to the company."

"I work hard, Mrs. Sneed."

"I saw you on television the other night. You're quite effective. You handle yourself well, Ben. Very photogenic, and I hear you're coming up in the world. . . bought yourself a new home in Albuquerque with a swimming pool. It's near the country club, isn't it?"

"Yes, it's nice."

"Choice property. You're popular Ben, and well thought of. I hear your name around Santa Fe and when I visit friends in Albuquerque. But tell me something?" asked Morgan, who lowered her voice as she glanced at guests several feet away. "Did you ever hear from that boy, the one who took. . . .?"

"Yes," said Ben in a hushed voice. "I received the. . . ."

"And destroyed them, I hope." Ben nodded in agreement. "How's your mother? You used to speak about her often."

"She's getting older. Can't hear too well, but she's holding her own."

"Does she still live in the house at Tesuque?" asked Morgan as she smiled at friends making their way toward the buffet.

"I paid for an addition to her home, and a new kitchen. It seems to make life easier for her."

"That was thoughtful," said Morgan as she glanced down at the blonde hairs which curled into circles on his broad, tanned chest. "Ever come up to Santa Fe?"

"Occasionally."

"Call me sometime, Ben. We'll do lunch, possibly dinner," said Morgan in a provocative tone before she turned and strolled into the kitchen.

By midnight the guests had gone. Ben walked Haley to her car, kissed her goodnight and returned to the empty portal. He wanted to tell Baxter his plans face to face. Sitting alone, he watched the lights of Los Alamos glimmer against the mountains, then heard Baxter call his name from the far end of the portal. Baxter seated himself on a bench beside the bar, then raised his sixth gin and tonic to his thin, pale lips. Ben crossed the portal, mixed a drink and settled next to Baxter, who glanced at Ben with a curious expression then asked, "What's this about, Ben? Can't it wait until Monday?"

"No, I don't think so," said Ben somberly. Baxter cut his bleary eyes to Ben who straightened before he continued. "I want you to know I appreciate everything you've done for me. I mean that."

"I'm grateful you told me. I'm proud of you. You've come a long way Ben, from planting flowers by our pool. You've done well. Your business reputation is impeccable. You've become a hot commodity. . . a young Native American who's intelligent and made a name for himself in the business community. Now what can't wait till Monday?"

Ben looked away and sipped the drink before he said, "I feel I need a new direction in my life. Something different. I've been approached recently."

Baxter turned sideways without taking his eyes off Ben. "You want to leave Sneed Oil?" he asked anxiously.

"No. I've been in meetings with some very influential people in the Republican party. I've been asked to run for political office." Stunned silence filled the portal. All Ben heard was the swish of cars on the Taos highway, then added, "They want my decision by tomorrow morning."

Baxter reached for his drink on the table. Several moments passed before he said in a rising tone, "I think that's wonderful, Ben. What office do they have in mind? A place on the Albuquerque city council? Better yet, a seat in the state legislature here in Santa Fe?"

Ben took in a deep breath before he said, "They want. . . ." Ben paused to clear his throat. "They want me to run for the United States Senate, to represent New Mexico."

Baxter's drink fell from his wrinkled hand and shattered on the portal. His hazel eyes locked on Ben, who glanced away at headlights streaming up the highway. Then Baxter said in his low, deep voice, "You're joking Ben? This can't be?"

"No, it's true. They've met with the higher-ups in Washington. They concluded my exposure all these years on television across New Mexico has given me a high enough profile, but mainly. . . ." Ben allowed the words to trail off as he stood to mix another drink. "But mainly, they believe a Native American can win the upcoming election. Win big. I'd be the first to be elected from New Mexico."

Baxter took his eyes off Ben and looked down at the shattered glass beside his shoe. "I don't know what to say, Ben. Of course I'm thrilled for you, but how will this affect your position with the company?"

"They said I'd have to quit. But if I'm defeated. . . ?"

Baxter stared into the darkness beyond the portal for several seconds. "I'll hire you back," he said in a distant manner as he struggled to his feet.

Baxter looked at Ben and thought of the first time he'd seen him standing by the gate, asking for a job to work the flower beds. His mind reached back to the young, innocent face, and the long blonde hair which needed cutting.

"Whatever I can do, Ben, just let me know," said Baxter in a sad voice as he steadied himself against the bench.

Ben reached out and placed his hand on Baxter's shoulder, then looked into his eyes. Baxter glanced away before Ben said quietly, "There's one thing I will need."

"What's that, Ben?"

"A campaign chairman. You've got contacts all over New Mexico and in Washington. You could be very influential in raising money for the campaign."

Baxter's eyes brightened before he eventually said, "Let me think about it. I've got a lot of irons in the fire right now. I've never been involved in politics."

"I've already spoken with the committee. They think you'd make a perfect chairman. You've got all the credentials."

The two men shook hands, then Ben turned and crossed the portal, walked through the zaguan, and out into the cool, night air. He stood quietly in the drive and watched the stars turn around the moon and he knew, like the night he'd first called Baxter from the phone booth, that there really was a God in heaven, holding up the stars above Tesuque.

By three the following afternoon, the switchboards at Sneed Oil were overwhelmed. In the parking lot, local television crews were aiming dishes from their vans in preparation for the announcement, scheduled at exactly one minute past five, mountain standard time. Earlier, the election committee had issued the news release at precisely the correct time, so the chances of Ben Touchstone's appearance on the local evening newscasts were rising by the minute. Two local stations had sent their anchors. NBC requested its affiliate feed the statement directly to New York so it could be aired on the evening news.

The committee was right, thought Ben, as he glanced from his window at the reporters, trucks and cameras filling the parking lot. He recalled what they'd said during their first meeting: "Ben, you'll seize the public's attention by storm. You'll be the first Native American to represent New Mexico in the Senate, plus you're only thirty, and to make it even more newsworthy, you're a Republican."

At five minutes before five, Ben made his way down the hall, followed closely by Baxter Sneed who joined him on the elevator, along with a publicist, the campaign manager and two of his assistants clutching papers in their hands.

Precisely at five o'clock, Ben straightened his tie and looked up into the glaring lights and microphones thrust into his face.

Fifty-five seconds later, Ben cleared his throat and stared into the cameras. "Fellow New Mexicans, my name is Benjamin Touchstone. I've called a news conference this afternoon to make, what to me, and for our state, is a momentous announcement." Ben paused, then swept his cobalt eyes across the lenses of the cameras. "It gives me great pleasure to announce, that I have accepted the Republican party's offer, and hope to be the first Native American to represent New Mexico in the Senate of the United States of America." Ben smiled broadly and heard the cameras click, then strobes flashed, and what seemed like a hundred questions thundered past his ears. He slowly raised his arms. "If you're wondering why I feel qualified to represent the divergent cultures of our state, then I'm proud to tell you I was born in an Indian pueblo just a few miles north of Santa Fe. My father is a full blood Tesuque Indian. My mother is an Anglo. I've come up from poverty, and was fortunate to have received a good education, then was offered a helping hand to become successful in business. In November, I will ask for your vote, and go to Washington owing no one any favors. I stand before you, a man proud to have the blood of two great cultures coursing through his veins. I will represent all of you, no matter what your color, or your beliefs. God bless our country and our state, and thank you from the bottom of my heart."

The clamor of questions was deafening. Baxter quickly stepped aside, then followed Ben and the entourage to the elevators. Moments later, Ben stood beside the mahogany desk in Baxter's office, smiling at the group which had stood in the background while the cameras captured every detail of his speech and appearance.

"You were wonderful, Ben," bubbled the campaign manager. His two assistants, still clutching papers, shook their heads in agreement. Baxter smiled, then poured himself a drink. The publicist scribbled a reminder for Ben to join the committee for a special dinner that night at the Hilton near the airport. He'd made certain the media would be there in full attendance.

From the leather chair in his living room, John Northcutt snapped the *Dallas Morning News* into shape and stared over the business page at the announcer in New York. He swirled the glass to mix the bourbon with the ice, then returned his attention to the local paper after hearing another war had broken out in a country he never knew existed.

Several moments passed, then a man's voice said, "It gives me great pleasure to announce. . . ." John sipped his drink as he continued to read about the falling price of oil. He glanced back at the screen when he heard, "The Republican party's offer. . . ." John froze, after the light complected, blue eyed man concluded, ". . . and I hope to be the first Native American to represent New Mexico in the Senate of the United States of America."

His mouth fell open as the paper slid to the carpet. He leaned forward, then saw Baxter Sneed smiling in the background, surrounded by reporters.

"Shit," he snapped, then lifted the telephone and punched in the sequence of numbers which connected him to the two-story town house in Georgetown.

"Sam? Did you hear what I just heard on NBC?"

"Yes, dammit. I thought you said I was running unopposed?"

"I don't know what to say. . . ."

"That half breed said it all—what the hell is going on? You said you had connections up here? How in hell didn't you know about this?" Without waiting for an answer, the junior senator from New Mexico continued, "I'm going to say this once, John. You listen closely. I've helped get some things passed for you up here, and your investments have done well by it. But I'm beginning to think you're not as well connected as you say you are."

"Sam, you've got to listen to me," said John, perched at the edge of the overstuffed chair. "This comes as a complete surprise. You'll see, when you hear what the Democratic leaders have to say about it. I want you to calm down. I have something to tell you. . . you have to keep this absolutely quiet," said John in a modulated voice. The young senator waited silently for what John Northcutt was about to say. "My son has in his possession a photographic negative of their candidate. Let's just say it involves him in a delicate situation with the wife. . . ." he lowered his voice further ". . . of someone very close to him. You must have seen him, the tall man—he was standing directly behind the candidate just now. He's his campaign chairman, Sam." John paused to sip the bourbon. "And another thing. My son also has a tape recording of the candidate accepting fifty thousand dollars for turning over copies of sensitive information from his company's files."

Silence fell between them until John asked, "Need I say more? Use your imagination, Sam."

"Good God!" exclaimed the senator. "But why does your son have them?"

"It was his idea. He hid the negative and the tape recording in the floorboard of his car. Pretty damn ingenious if you ask me."

"Do whatever you have to do," said the senator in a somber tone. But if I have to run against this. . . ."

"Calm down, Sam, like I said, we have the negative and the tape. You need to trust me more," said John with optimism as he replaced the receiver then smiled and crossed the room toward the bar.

Earlier the same day, from his home by the eighteenth green of the Albuquerque Country Club, Ben had placed the call to Kate, informing her of his candidacy. Amelia had also phoned, as well as Father Ortiz, who'd called her from the hospital. Luther had dropped by and stayed for quite awhile to watch the televised reports. That evening, during a banquet at the Hilton, Ben delivered another speech before the cameras, which was even more impressive than the one he'd given in the parking lot at five that afternoon.

It had finally begun and Ben let out a long, deep sigh before he switched off the reading light beside his bed. It would be a tough road ahead, he knew, the hardest road he'd ever walked.

Before he fell asleep, Ben recalled what the angel had told him in the chapel at Chimayo, "I'll always be with you."

In a single week, Touchstone had become a household name throughout the state. From the tiny town of La Mesilla which borders Texas to Chama in the north, Ben had become a topic of conversation at dinner tables, barbershops and offices across New Mexico.

Standing on the platform beside the obelisk, Ben's eyes swept across the crowd which filled the plaza in Santa Fe. He smoothed the silk tie, then secured the middle button of his gray, tweed jacket. Placing both hands firmly on the podium, he glanced quickly at the ending of the speech he had written only minutes before appearing on the platform.

"As I've said before, New Mexico is unique. We have more minorities than almost any other state in this great country, but until now, our divergent voices have been just a whisper. But come November, things will be very different in Washington." He paused for applause erupting from the crowd which spilled from the plaza into the streets and sidewalks, even past the shops on San Francisco Street to the steps of the Cathedral. Ben smiled, then resumed in a strong, clear voice, as clear as the azure sky above the plaza.

"My fellow New Mexicans, when I was thirteen, I can proudly say I attended the Indian School here in Santa Fe. The very first day we were given candles as we walked into the gymnasium for an assembly. An old man appeared, an elder from San Juan Pueblo, who spoke in a low, firm voice. His name was Oku Pin, which means Turtle Mountain in the Tewa language. I'll never forget what he said that morning after the room was plunged into darkness. He told us to light our candles as our tribe's names were called. As he continued down the list, more and more flames appeared. When he concluded, several hundred small, brown faces were framed by the glow of candles. Then he said to us, `Now you see what we can do. Come together as family. Stand together and light the way for each of us.' I ask all of you to stand together in the coming election. Vote with your heart, not just for a political party. Now is the time for all of us— Anglos, Hispanics and Native Americans to come together. This is what I offer you when I take my place in Washington. Thank you for being here, and may God bless us all."

The applause quickly swelled into a roar of cheers echoing off the buildings surrounding the plaza. Strobe lights flashed, then video camera lenses tightened on his broad smile and the shock of blonde hair hanging limp above his cobalt eyes.

Ben stood motionless for several minutes, waving at the crowd pressing around the platform. In the shade beneath an elm tree near the corner of the plaza, Baxter applauded. In Tesuque, Kate lowered the volume of the television, smiled, then wiped a tear from her clouded, gray eyes. Father Ortiz, propped in bed at the hospital, glanced at the crucifix on the bedside table and said a prayer for Ben, who continued to wave at the people and the cameras. At that moment, he saw her face, wedged between reporters clamoring for his attention. Pilar pushed closer and shouted, "Evangelo's," then pointed to the small bar, a hundred feet from the corner of the plaza.

Thirty minutes later, Ben glanced up at the hand lettered sign, then stepped into the dimly lit bar. Cigarette smoke hung in layers above the booths and the tables draped with yellowed plastic cloths. Above the booths, thatched palm leaves lent a curious ambience to the room. Ben blinked in the shadows, then saw Pilar facing the jukebox, a can of beer between her fingers. Her long black hair hung straight, almost touching the concha belt cinched around her slender waist. Her tight jeans outlined a lean, contoured figure. She turned and motioned to the booth beside the jukebox. Ben walked slowly past the tables. A large Hispanic man, sitting by himself, glanced sideways at Ben from under the brim of a wide, straw hat. The odor of stale beer permeated the small, dark room and as Ben drew closer, he watched Pilar, now seated in the booth, lift the can of beer and smile. Smoke curled past her olive colored eyes.

"Hello, Ben. It's been awhile," Pilar said with a hardness in her voice as she crushed the cigarette in the thin metal ashtray by her elbow.

Ben halted, turned, then saw Henry, his back propped against the booth facing Pilar, who lit another cigarette. Ben fell silent as he studied his brother: the gaunt face, his unkept hair which touched the collar of his undershirt.

His dark eyes held a dull expression. Then Henry hunched his thin shoulders and moved the shot glass closer to his mouth. Ben stared in disbelief at Henry who straightened, then looked across the table at Pilar, who said quietly, "Sit down, Ben, we need to talk."

Ben glanced at the man behind the bar who was talking on the telephone before he settled beside Henry who lit a cigarette, coughed, then motioned for another round of drinks. No one spoke for several moments until Henry said in a caustic tone, "I guess you're famous now? Got the whole state talking about you. Kate should be proud."

Ben glanced sideways at Henry, then to Pilar, her eyes fixed on the can of beer.

"Yes, as a matter of fact, she is. Henry, you've lost a lot of weight. You don't look well. Have you seen a doctor?"

Ben watched Henry pull a hundred dollar bill from his jeans and hand it to the bartender, who leaned and placed slices of lemon, a shot glass of tequila and a beer in the center of the table. As Henry lifted the glass, Ben said cautiously, "Mother said you'd lost your job."

"Which one? I've gotten fired several times lately. Want to hear about it?" asked Henry with sarcasm as he sucked on the lemon before downing the tequila.

"Where'd you get the money, Henry? You just paid with a hundred dollar bill."

"A friend. He helps me out when I'm running low."

"Anyone I know? Is he from the pueblo?"

Henry laughed.

"What's so amusing?"

"Yeah, you know him. Said he wants to talk to you."

Ben let out a sigh, loosened his tie then turned and said to Henry, "You know I worry about you. Besides Kate, you're the only family I've got. If you asked me here to argue, I'm not interested. You need money? I'll loan you some, but Henry, you haven't tried to help yourself. Mother still worries about you. You're a grown man, Henry. Act like one."

Henry continued to stare at the empty glass suspended from his fingers which began to tremble as he fumbled for a cigarette. Pilar struck a match. Henry exhaled and let the smoke curl around his nostrils which flared as he cut his eyes to Ben and blurted out, "You're gonna lose, Ben."

"What? What are you saying?"

"I said you're gonna lose the election. Something's gonna happen. It's gonna be in all the papers but my friend said for me to keep my mouth shut. I've said too much already."

Pilar watched Ben's lips tighten before he said, "Henry, you told me once that you vowed to bring me down. Is this it? It will destroy mother. She hasn't many years left, Henry. Whatever you've planned, at least wait until the election's over. Don't deny her this. For the first time in her life, she's happy and proud. If you do whatever it is you're threatening, it will cost you—believe me, more than you can imagine. We will settle it later between ourselves. Just the two of us in the garden behind the house. Have I made myself clear?"

Ben watched Henry's mouth twist into a smile before he drained the final drop of tequila from the glass. Pilar looked away, afraid of meeting Ben's eyes.

Ben stood and stared down at Henry sucking on the lemon rind. He caught himself before he spoke again, then turned and walked quickly through the door and out into the cool, crisp air and brilliant light of the plaza.

SEVENTEEN

Weeks passed quickly, then autumn arrived without notice from Ben who was too busy meeting people in every town he could get to. Baxter Sneed's private plane never rested and donations which Baxter raised continued to pour in from across the state and beyond. Ben had become an overnight sensation. He crisscrossed New Mexico, determined to bring a needed change to politics. As far as he was concerned, the old boy network of special interest groups was halfway under water, drowning fast.

USA Today had featured him on the front page. Even *Newsweek* and *Time* sent reporters to interview the intriguing candidate from the obscure pueblo north of Santa Fe.

It was now the day of the election and Ben was anxious. The latest polls reported he was leading the incumbent by a healthy margin. At Ben's request, Luther met him at his office, then drove with him to party headquarters at the Hilton near the airport.

Ben watched the hour hand on the clock hanging above the stage in the ballroom creep toward seven. In forty-five minutes, the polls would close and returns would begin flooding in. Ben sipped coffee at the end of a long table draped with banners as large screen televisions blared from the corners of the room. People swirled around him, but he could only watch the clock as he silently prayed. The television anchors rattled off the returns, declaring the election tied. More returns would follow through the evening. Camera lights swept the cavernous room, filled with supporters, friends, and the media which closed around him like a shell around a pearl.

By six thirty he was exhausted and excused himself to be alone and rest for half an hour in his upstairs suite, high above the noise.

In the lobby, Ben pushed the button and waited for the elevator. Moments later he walked slowly down the hall toward the suite. The floor was quiet, a relief from the clamor of the ballroom. He fumbled for his keys, unlocked the door and moved with fatigue across the thick, green carpet. He stopped to pull the drapes and stared out at the snow gliding past the window. It was the same kind of snowfall, many years ago on Christmas Eve, the week after Ojo had deserted them. His mind reached back to when he, Kate and Henry made the steep climb toward Chimayo. Then he thought of his angel and how real she appeared that night in the room beside the altar.

He turned abruptly as the phone rang. "Yes?"

Standing in the lobby, his publicist covered the mouthpiece and said in a whisper, "There's a woman down here who says she's got something crucial to tell you. She claims it's personal. Says it could determine the outcome of the election."

"Oh?"

"I think you need to see her. Shall I send her up?"

Ben slumped into the sofa and waited. There was a soft knock at the door. He crossed the room, turned the knob and was surprised to find Pilar Ocate standing in the hall.

"Pilar! Has something happened to Henry?"

"I have something for you. Close the door," she whispered as she slipped past Ben into the room as he locked and chained the door.

"What is it? Can't this wait until. . . .?" Ben stopped in mid-sentence as Pilar slowly drew a photograph from the cleavage of her low cut dress and handed it to Ben. Color drained from his face as he stared at the picture of Morgan Sneed.

"Where in hell did you get this?" he gasped.

"From your friend who took it. He kept a negative for himself. He also said to tell you he has a tape recording."

"A tape recording?" asked Ben in disbelief.

"Yes, he said you'd remember. There was a man who came to your office and offered you fifty thousand dollars. You took the money Ben, remember? He said your conversation was recorded."

Ben's legs began to tremble as he steadied himself against the wall. Sweat formed in his palms. "That bastard Northcutt. What does he want?"

"Harry wants you to withdraw from the election, before all the returns are in. You could still do it. You have thirty minutes. If you don't, he said he'll give the picture and the tape recording to the newspapers at nine o'clock tonight."

"Why is he doing this?"

"Harry said it's important to his father."

"How the hell did you meet him?"

"He's been hanging around the pueblo. He and I got together a few times before I moved in with Henry."

"How much is he paying you to do this?"

"Henry and I need the money."

"So this is what Henry was talking about?"

"Sure. He jokes about it. Says you're finally going to get what you deserve."

Ben walked toward the sofa. Moments later Pilar called his name. He turned to find her standing nude, clothes in piles around her feet. She moved slowly toward him, then said in a deep, peculiar voice, "I've always wanted you Ben. You're the only one I've ever wanted. Remember that Christmas morning, when we were alone in your house and almost. . . ."

"Stop, Pilar, this has gone far enough. Get dressed. Someone could walk in here any second."

"No, Ben, you've locked and chained the door, remember?" Ben stared at her soft, full breasts, then down to her flat stomach and long dark legs.

"Ben, I know where the negative is, and the tape. One night Harry and I got drunk and he told me where he hid them. If you make love to me, I'll tell you where they are." Suddenly, the phone rang on the table near the sofa.

"Don't answer it Ben. Look at me. Don't you want to touch me?" asked Pilar in a guttural tone as she drew closer.

"Hello? Who is this?" snapped Ben who turned to watch Pilar's long dark tongue move closer to his neck. "Who is this?" he repeated, then saw her face twist into something strange and hideous. Ben stared at her eyes which glowed like hot, molten rubies. Startled, he moved slowly backward then heard the man ask, "Am I speaking with Ben Touchstone?"

"Yes, what is it?" Ben felt Pilar's cold fingers touch his face, then her arms locked around his waist.

"This is Sergeant Ortega in Española with the state police. I have very bad news for you, sir. There's been a terrible accident. Your brother Henry is dead." Ben pushed away from Pilar and dropped to the sofa as Ortega continued. "We found his body, along with another man and a woman on the Taos highway. All three were killed instantly. Collided with a truck. We found an empty liquor bottle by their car. The car was engulfed in flames when we arrived."

"Are you sure?" asked Ben in a weak voice.

"Yes sir, all three bodies were positively identified by the coroner."

"When did this happen?"

"This afternoon, around five."

"You're positive about the time?"

"Yes sir, I was there. I wrote up the report."

"Who was in the car with my brother?" asked Ben, his words barely audible.

"The owner of the Porsche was identified as Harry Northcutt from Dallas."

"And the woman?"

"Her drivers license listed her as Pilar Ocate, from Tesuque."

The phone fell from his hand as a sharp chill shot down his spine and his eyes swept the empty room. The door was still locked and chained. He stared down at where she'd dropped her clothes, but they were gone. Then he smelled a foul, pungent odor.

Ben retrieved the phone and in a shaken voice stammered, "I have to go."

Ben put down the phone as tears of confusion flooded his face. He sobbed uncontrollably. Suddenly, the lights flickered off and engulfed in darkness, Ben dropped to his knees.

"Ben?" The voice seemed to come from the hallway. He lifted his head and groped his way toward the door.

"Ben? Are you there?" Ben struggled to his feet. In the blackness, he moved cautiously toward the voice as the scent of roses filled the room.

Blindly, he stumbled backward—then suddenly, a hot flash of silver light rushed toward him. Ben shut his eyes to the brightness. He froze as something brushed his shoulder. He opened his eyes and watched in awe as the light raced across the room, then whipped into a ball which seemed to spin wildly above his head. Before he could turn away, the orb shot toward the ceiling, then quietly transformed into the figure of his angel, her clear, indigo eyes smiling down at him. Terrified, Ben struggled for breath. His heart pounded. He tried to speak but the figure raised her fingers to her lips. His breathing became erratic as he backed away.

"Be calm, Ben, there's nothing to be afraid of," she said softly. Terrified, he glanced around the darkened room. The angel smiled again and moved her hand.

Suddenly Nando appeared and walked toward Ben. His eyes were translucent, like water. His body glowed in the darkness, and Ben could see every detail of his being. Nando smiled gently, then handed Ben a tulip bulb, exactly like the one he'd given him in the greenhouse years before. He said to Ben in his deep, warm voice, "Plant it Ben. I hope it reminds you of all the things we talked about. It will always bloom, but only if you keep your thoughtfulness for others alive and growing in your heart." Stunned, Ben studied the gnarled root before it fell from his fingers to the carpet. His eyes followed the radiant figure as Nando settled in a chair beside the table.

The angel gently moved her hand again and pointed to an empty chair across from Nando. Ben was oblivious to the phone ringing on the table beside the sofa. Two Crows quietly materialized, his soft, gray eyes staring back at Ben in silence. Ben covered his face and turned away but Two Crows stood and slowly crossed the darkened room, then leaned and snapped a silver chain and cross around Ben's neck.

"You lost it, Ben, remember? In a flower bed on Circle Drive. I want you to have it to remember me and how I helped you. Soon you will be able to help many other people."

Ben's dry lips parted as he struggled to speak. "You saved my life, Two Crows. I'll never forget it. You saved Kate's life too, the night you frightened Ojo from the house. She told me later," Ben said in a tense voice as Two Crows slowly returned to the table.

The phone rang again but Ben remained transfixed. His skin tingled as he watched the angel glide across the carpet, then float in the air beside the window. She slowly bowed her head as Luther materialized. His legs were folded as he sat quietly on the floor beside the sofa. He lit a smudge stick and moved it over his face, then past his deep-set eyes which were fixed on Ben. Luther stood and moved closer, then reached into the pocket of his jeans. "Ben, remember when you asked me what I carried in my medicine bag?"

"Yes, Luther," Ben answered, almost choking on his words. "When we were on our way to fish the canyon. You told me to be patient, that someday you might give it to me."

"That day has come, Ben." Luther opened his dark, thin fingers and handed Ben the small leather pouch. "Look inside, Ben." Ben cautiously reached into the bag and studied the dried sprigs of cedar he cradled in his trembling hands.

"Ben, when you smell the cedar, think of the forests which need protection. The trees, rivers, animals, mountains. . . all things have souls. It will soon be in your power to stop the ruthless destruction of Mother Earth. Do it for all human beings. Now look into the bag again."

Ben slowly extracted the caddis fly and held it between his fingers.

"That's the fly you used, years ago, to catch the trout in Cundiyo canyon. The big one, the one you gave back to the river. You spared its life, Ben. It was a very noble thing you did. Let that fly remind you of the respect people should have for all living things. Everything's a gift from God. But there's one more thing, Ben, at the bottom of the bag."

Ben's quivering fingers touched the moist red clay, then brought it closer to his face.

"That's soil from our pueblo, Ben, to remind you of our own people who are still ignored and rejected by the world. The clay is where you came from Ben and someday will return. Hold all these things inside your heart, for soon you will be given the authority to make an impact on the world."

The angel moved through the air and floated by the door. Her eyes glowed like blue-white stars, then she smiled and bowed her head.

Suddenly, the lights flickered on as the phone began to ring. Ben slowly lifted the receiver and heard Baxter's voice, barely audible through the clamor in the ballroom.

"Ben, I called you twice, but no one answered. I started to come up to your room. Were you asleep?"

"No, I was very much awake. What is it?"

"You've won, Ben," he shouted. "Can you hear me? You've won."

Ben studied the snow gliding past the window. He quietly replaced the phone, reached for the leather pouch, held it for a moment then dropped it in his pocket as he moved toward the door.